Rosewood Place

CORPSES &
CONMEN

RUBY BLAYLOCK

Ruby Blaylock

Corpses & Conmen

Contents

1

Anxiously Awaiting

Annie Richards smoothed her dress down for what felt like the millionth time that morning. She pulled her hair up in a casual ponytail, then pulled it back down again, unable to choose between comfort and looking somewhat professional. The phrase 'first impressions' bounced around the inside of her head like a rubber ball, but she reminded herself that, as the owner of her very own business and the master of her own destiny, she could make whatever type of impression she wanted, as long as it wasn't a bad one.

She peered out of the window in the parlour, staring down the driveway as though doing so might hurry things along somewhat. A quick glance at the grandfather clock behind her told her that it was early still--her first guest would likely be another hour away, at least, but the knowledge of that fact didn't settle the butterflies in her stomach. Normally Annie thought of herself as a patient person, but today, waiting felt like it took forever.

She flitted around Rosewood Place like an insect, inspecting nooks and crannies for dust or out-of-place items. She helped her mother in the kitchen hoping that the distraction of preparing snacks for her guests would help alleviate her nerves, but it didn't quite do the job. All Annie could focus on was the fact that Rosewood Place was opening its doors to its very first guests, and by some miracle, it was fully booked.

Rory Jenkins passed by one of the large windows on the front of the house. He carried a hammer in one hand and a toolbox in the other. After spending months working on renovating the plantation style farmhouse, he'd become part of the scenery. Originally, Rory was meant to be a contractor, hired just long enough to whip the place into something suitable for use as a bed-and-breakfast. After Annie's mother, Bessie, worked her charms on Rory, pleading with him to stick around and help keep the place in good working order, he'd agreed to take on the role of full-time handyman for the grand old house.

Annie knew he hadn't taken the job for the money; the business was a long way from profitable right then. And he hadn't taken it for lack of work. Rory had developed a reputation as a fine carpenter and fair tradesman who took great pride in doing a good job. She suspected that Rory's love of the house's history played some part in his decision, and her mother seemed convinced that Annie and Rory's own history played some part as well. They'd dated for nearly three years in high school and had been friends long before that. She often wondered how differently her life would have been if Rory hadn't ended their relationship after graduation, but she knew it didn't do to dwell on the past.

Annie cast her mind back to the early part of the year when she'd been unsure of whether she'd be able to pull off a challenge as big as renovating the old farmhouse. She often felt that she'd overcome so much in the past year that she'd practically been transformed into an entirely new person. Perhaps she'd actually turned into the old Annie, the one who'd been headstrong and determined, who'd never been afraid to tackle a challenge. That Old Annie was who she'd been before she got married and moved to the Big Apple. Twenty years of marriage to someone who cared more about the appearance of their marriage than the actual state of it left her feeling lost and somewhat incapable, at least for a little while.

Annie had become a widow at the age of forty and had discovered that her late husband had been quite the liar and cheat during their marriage. She had decided almost immediately to reclaim her life with her sixteen-year-old son back in the welcoming folds of Coopersville, South Carolina. After some time spent acclimating to life in a small town, Devon had learned to love the place almost as much as his mother, and with the help of Annie's own mother, Bessie, they'd turned Annie's dream of opening a country inn into a reality.

Annie looked around her and smiled. The farmhouse looked very different than it had when she'd first bought it. It had been empty for several years when she'd first set foot inside the antebellum home. Originally built sometime in the late 1700's, it had grown and changed with each new owner, beginning as a shanty on a hundred acres of farmland and blooming into an enormous farmhouse on ten meagre acres of land. As a plantation, Rosewood Place had failed miserably, or so Annie thought. What should have been a huge success never seemed to thrive as a functioning plantation. Crops failed and the Cooper family, who owned the plantation during its most successful years, couldn't even afford to keep the slaves needed to farm the place.

The view from the windows at the front of the house was beautiful and somehow calming. Annie spent a great deal of time on the front porch just outside these windows admiring the gentle slope of the lawn that stretched lazily down to the main road. Her gravel driveway, which had been recently filled with new white gravel to fill the crevices created from rain washing down the hill, stood out in stark contrast to the shadows of the trees that lined one side and the stubby green grass that lined the other.

Wildflowers and dandelions dotted the edge of the lawn where Annie hadn't been able to bring herself to cut them. She noted with some satisfaction that the blackberry bushes still held a handful of fat berries. They'd be dried up and bitter in a few days but Annie had already picked more than enough for several pies and a few jars of jam. Her mother had frozen some as well, so they'd enjoy them long into the fall. These last berries were for the birds, of which there were many out here in the South Carolina countryside. Annie loved watching them from her porch, where the sound of cars driving along the main road could hardly be heard. Rosewood Place felt so cozy, so lost from the world around it, that Annie sometimes forgot that anywhere else existed at all. She hoped that her guests would feel this way, too.

Annie was glad that the plantation had been a failure. If it had thrived, she probably would have never been able to afford the place, and because Annie hated the idea of slavery, she would have felt guilty living in a place where human beings were regularly mistreated and abused. No, it was definitely one of those lucky, beautiful coincidences that this particular farm had slipped into near oblivion. The universe had lined everything up perfectly to ensure that Annie and her little family wound up here, and for that, she was grateful.

Tearing herself away from the window, Annie made her way into the large sitting room at the front of the house. It was one of two sitting rooms, the other was the small parlour at the main entrance of the home, and it was one of Annie's favorite rooms in the house. Windows lined two walls, letting in plenty of natural light. There was an enormous fireplace, which, much to her delight, had required only a thorough cleaning to make it fully functional. She envisioned cozy winter evenings by the fire with her guests and family members, sipping cocoa and eating her mother's homemade chocolate chip cookies.

Several oversized chairs dotted the perimeter of the room. They were comfy and inviting, perfect for piling up with a book on a lazy afternoon. Annie crossed the sitting room and pushed open a small door in the far right corner. It was designed to blend in with the wall on which it hung, giving it the appearance of a section of panelling. This 'hidden' door swung open to reveal a tiny room filled wall-to-wall with books. It had originally been some sort of storage room or possibly an oversized closet, but Rory had insisted that a grand plantation house ought to have at least a small library, and he'd dutifully fitted it with floor-to-ceiling shelves. Annie had contributed some of her own books to the library, and her mother had added a few of her own. The rest were purchased at the annual Friends of the Library sale back in June.

Annie smiled as she recalled her son picking out a handful of books for younger guests. He'd been almost too shy to pay for them when he'd seen that the girl behind the library counter was young and pretty. Annie suspected that Devon's recently increased appetite for reading had quite a lot to do with the young library assistant, and she silently hoped that he was on his way to making some friends his own age here in town.

She knew that once school started in a few weeks Devon would have less time for her and likely less interest in working at the inn.

At sixteen, he still didn't have his driver's license, and she made a mental note to try and remedy that before his next birthday. She dreaded seeing him become so independent, but at the same time, she was extremely proud of how mature he'd become these past few months.

She supposed that letting him have a say in certain aspects of his new home and their family business had directly contributed to that newfound maturity. She'd put Devon in charge of designing his own attic room, and despite her worries that he'd turn it into some sort of high-tech bachelor pad, Annie was pleasantly surprised by Devon's design choices. She suspected that Rory may have had a hand in steering him towards a room that was practical and that fit with the house's history, though Devon's personal touch was clearly seen in the small details. She knew of no other plantation-era home that had a TARDIS-style closet built into its attic, but she decided that she could live with that quirk quite happily.

Annie ran her fingers across the spines of the books in the tiny library and pulled one from the shelf. It was a history book about Coopersville that she'd bought from the local history museum. There was very little about Rosewood Place, the plantation on which her home had been built, but there was plenty of information about the rest of her small hometown. She stepped out of the library and closed the door behind her before placing the history book on the coffee table in front of a pair of plush armchairs. Her guests would likely find the history book to be a charming touch, and it would give them an idea of what the rest of the town was like, if they were interested.

A small table and two chairs sat in front of one of the large windows facing out to the side of the house. Annie grinned as she noted the deck of playing cards her mother had placed on it along with a glass candy dish filled to the brim with peppermint candies. Bessie loved a good game of cards, and Annie wouldn't be surprised if her mother spent time trying to convince their guests to play a few hands with her. Bessie could be quite persuasive at times, especially if she really wanted something. Annie was secretly relieved that her mother would finally have someone other than herself and Rory to play with, since Devon flatly refused to learn any of her 'old woman' card games.

As if Bessie knew that her daughter was thinking about her, she appeared suddenly and silently beside her. "Are you still fussing over this room? I told you, it's perfect."

Annie jumped. "How do you move so quietly? I swear, Mother, one of these days you are going to give me a heart attack!"

Bessie grinned. "I guess it's just my natural, catlike abilities," she teased. "You know, I may be on my way to becoming a septuagenarian, but I'm not dead yet, just in case you thought I was some sort of ghost." Bessie loved to tease her daughter about ghosts, especially ones that might lurk inside the walls of a home that was over two-hundred years old. Although they had yet to experience any ghostly experiences, Annie couldn't help but let her imagination run away with her. If she actually did see a ghost, she'd probably faint from fright, but Annie doubted it would make her stop loving her new home.

Bessie also loved pointing out that she was 'getting on in years,' though she hadn't actually hit her seventies yet and was as fit as many women half her age. Despite hair that was white as snow, Bessie didn't look her age, either. She had a cheerful, slightly chubby face and the soft curves and edges that a grandmother was supposed to have. She did have a touch of arthritis, but unless it was very cold or rainy it didn't seem to slow her down. Her favorite walking stick, which had been a gift from Annie's late father, was brought out every now and then, used more for show than out of any actual necessity.

Annie suspected that her mother loved making people underestimate her abilities. Whether this was because Bessie liked to shock others with what she could actually do, or whether she just liked to play the helpless little old lady, Annie wasn't entirely sure. She'd just accepted it as a personality quirk of her mother's that she could live with. Bessie might claim to be some helpless old lady, but her active social life and vigorous domestic activities painted a very different picture.

Bessie was often up before everyone else, cooking and cleaning cheerfully until the rest of her family was up and active. She'd begged Rory to build her both a chicken coop and a large garden, though Annie drew the line at allowing Bessie to have a dairy cow.

"It's a farmhouse, Annie. We need farm animals," Bessie had protested.

"It's a bed-and-breakfast, Mother. We need beds and food," Annie had retorted before acquiescing to the chickens.

Now they stood in the doorway to the sitting room, each smiling as they imagined the guests who would get to enjoy the room as much as they had these past months. "It's going to be mighty fine, Annie. You wait and see."

Annie followed her mother into the kitchen and poured herself a glass of iced tea. She eyed the trays of finger sandwiches that Bessie had prepared that morning. The trays filled an entire shelf of their oversized refrigerator. Beside the fridge, rows of cupcakes stood at attention, frosted in vanilla and chocolate buttercream. Bessie was an enthusiastic cook who loved to bake as well, so it seemed only natural that she take on the cooking duties at the B&B. Annie knew she'd have to take on more of the cooking responsibilities later on, but for now, Bessie had things firmly under control.

Bessie ran a hand across her white hair, patting the bun on top of her head gently before pushing her spectacles up on the bridge of her nose. She'd had white hair as long as Annie could remember. Apparently, it was common in Bessie's family for the women to go prematurely grey, but Annie took after her father's side of the family and she only found the rare sliver of a grey hair hiding in her chestnut locks.

Robert Purdy had been buried with very little grey in his thick brown mop. Annie only wished that her father's heart had been as virile as his hair, but he'd been gone for over five years now. Like her husband, her father had suffered a massive heart attack and died suddenly. Unlike Annie's husband, David, her father had died in his sleep while napping in his recliner. David had died at work, or rather, in the ambulance on the way to the hospital. Both deaths had shaken her to her core, but of the two men, Annie could honestly say she missed her father the most.

"Annie, let's set up a little buffet table out in the back room, the one that overlooks the pond," Bessie suggested, pulling Annie from her reverie. "We can put some ice out there to keep the cold foods chilled and turn the fans on to get a breeze going."

The back room Bessie referred to was actually a veranda that had been screened in. Annie had considered having actual windows installed and turning the porch into another room of the house, but it was so charming as it was, she hated to change it. It ran most of the length of the back side of the house, and although it was narrow, it felt much larger because of the clean white walls and large, airy screens that overlooked the back of her property. From the veranda, she could see most of the pond, the back part of her barn, and her mother's little chicken coop.

The view from the screened in porch was peaceful enough, but Rory had taken things to another level by restoring the little boat dock on the edge of the pond and expanding it to include a large wooden deck that overlooked the pond. A gravel pathway connected the deck to the screened in porch. Annie felt it was absolutely perfect and she often took her coffee out to the little deck to bask in the quiet of an early morning in the countryside. After spending nearly two decades living in New York City, she couldn't be happier to find herself living in the middle of nowhere.

Annie helped her mother set up two folding tables on the veranda and then draped tablecloths over them. *Simple, but elegant*, she hoped. She helped her mother bring out dish after dish until the spread was complete. Annie returned to the kitchen just in time to see a van pull up the long driveway in front of the house. The butterflies returned to Annie's stomach with a vengeance as the vehicle pulled to a stop. Her first guest had arrived and he'd brought an entire news crew with him.

2

The First Guests Arrive

"Annie Richards?" The man climbing out of the passenger side of the van looked vaguely familiar. Annie wracked her brain trying to figure out where she'd seen him before, but he beat her to it. "I'm Rob Reynolds from WCOP news. Are you Mrs. Richards?"

Realization of who Rob Reynolds was made Annie's cheeks flush. He was one of the newscasters on the morning news program that her mother watched. From what Annie could recall, he covered community events and 'fluff' pieces, but he was a very popular television personality in the small town of Coopersville. He flashed a dazzling white smile at her and ran his fingers through jet black, perfectly coiffed hair. *Quite the charmer*, she mused.

Recovering her senses, Annie replied. "Yes, I'm Annie Richards, but I'm a little confused--didn't I book you in as a guest?" She gestured to the van and the accompanying cameraman. "Did I miss something when we spoke on the phone?"

Annie wasn't happy about being ambushed by a cameraman, but she listened as Rob explained why he'd brought Chris, the man behind the camera. "Your new bed-and-breakfast is kind of a big deal," he explained. "I mean, you took a crumbling wreck of a farmhouse and transformed it into this--" he gestured towards her home, "amazing B&B. It's a great human interest story, too. I have to say that I truly admire you for coming home from New York to take on such a monumental task while you're no doubt still mourning the loss of your husband."

Annie's stomach did a little dropkick. "How do you know all this?" She could feel perspiration prickling at the back of her neck and couldn't decide if it was from the heat or the shock of having a complete stranger know so much about her.

Rob blushed. "It's my job, Mrs. Richards."

She took a deep breath, then remembered that they were standing in the August heat. "Why don't we go inside and get you checked in, Mr. Reynolds. That is, if you are planning to stay here overnight."

Relief flooded the news anchor's face. "Yes, ma'am. And I'm sorry, I know I should have mentioned the possibility that they'd send a cameraman with me--"

"They?" she asked, leading the two men up the stairs on the front porch.

"The station, my bosses," he explained. "Originally, I was supposed to just come for a stay and write up an editorial piece, sort of a combination of review and a look at the home's history. I'm trying to take on more journalistic style work," he added, "but I genuinely do want to stay at your lovely home. At the last minute, my boss decided to send Chris here to get a little footage. He'll be leaving after he takes a little tour, and after my stay, I'll do a review on the community segment of the Saturday morning newscast. It's free publicity for you," he added sheepishly.

Annie ushered the men into the parlour where the cool air of a discreetly air-conditioned house greeted them. Annie had agonized over whether or not to keep the home as close to its original state as possible, but the brutal summer temperatures swayed her. She'd found a way to tastefully disguise the central heat and air unit behind the house and Rory had helped her source elegant vent covers that didn't stick out like a sore thumb.

"Would you gentlemen like a cold drink before I give you a tour of the property?" Annie glanced past them to the kitchen. Bessie stood in the doorway, grinning like a cat that had just swallowed a rather tasty birdie.

Before they could answer, Bessie appeared with two glasses of freshly squeezed lemonade. Annie led them into the sitting room and left the men with her mother, who was happy to discuss the home and its history at length. Annie stifled a laugh as she headed to the little room that led off behind the parlour. Whatever information the reporter and his cameraman hoped to learn about the house, Bessie would certainly share with them, and more. She reckoned that they'd regret engaging with her mother on the topic of the house because she would, without a doubt, talk their ears off.

Annie opened the door to her office. It was a fairly small room, only about twenty by fifteen feet in size, but large enough for a small desk and filing cabinet. She also kept a locked box containing every room key for the house as well as the keys for the barn, the small tractor that she'd bought to keep the brush cleared away, and the spare keys to the storage building that she'd had erected out behind the barn.

Rory had teased her for building a storage shed while she had a perfectly good, perfectly empty barn standing, but she swore that by the next summer she would have the barn transformed into a party venue. When he explained the costs to her, she almost faltered, but she reminded him that just a few bookings each season would help them recover the cost pretty quickly. For now, the barn was her lowest priority, and she was almost embarrassed by how hard she'd worked Rory over the past few months trying to get Rosewood Place open before summer's end. Fortunately, he seemed to love Rosewood Place as much as she did, so she pushed her guilt aside and instead learned to tackle some of the repairs herself so she could ease Rory's workload just a little.

Unfortunately, Annie was a disaster with a hammer, but she found that she could sand, paint, and stain like a pro, so she'd taken on a great deal of the cosmetic repairs while Rory had tackled the complex tasks. He'd taken Devon on as an apprentice of sorts, teaching the teen how to do some of the easier woodworking projects on his own. "Might as well learn from me," Rory had explained. "I've heard that woodworking class is a thing of the past."

Annie thought about how much Devon had learned from Rory already this past summer, and as she pulled Rob's room key from the lock box she wondered how Devon would find the small high school that he'd be attending in a few short weeks. She thought of her own time there decades before, and as she locked the box back up she made a mental note to go online and check to see when she could expect the school supplies that she'd ordered to arrive. Annie had wised up to the benefits of back to school shopping online so she didn't have to battle the crowds in search of a bargain in the crowded aisles at the local MegaMart.

Annie was surprised to find that two more guests had arrived while she'd been in the office, and while she chatted with the pair, a lovely married couple who'd come all the way from Ohio, two more arrived. Within the space of a little over an hour, Annie's big, empty home filled up with more guests than she could have imagined.

Doris and Frank Martin made themselves comfortable on the

sitting room sofa, sipping lemonade and cooing over every detail of the renovated room. Doris seemed to have a keen interest in the books Annie had left out for the guests to peruse, so Bessie told her all about the hidden library. Annie couldn't help but smile at how quickly Bessie and Doris seemed to hit it off. Doris and her husband were both in their sixties and the bubbly woman had explained that with retirement looming, they wanted to see if South Carolina was the kind of place that they'd like to retire.

Hailing from Ohio, the married couple seemed fascinated by the old house and the rolling fields surrounding it. Frank's eyes twinkled when Bessie told him that there was a fully stocked pond out behind the house and fishing poles in the storage shed. Doris practically beamed when Bessie promised to show her the hidden library and tunnel that ran the length of the house, a feature leftover from the house's early days as a slave-worked plantation.

Alexander George was a quiet, mousy man who seemed to appear from nowhere, slipping into the sitting room with his single bag and watery eyes. He stood in one corner until Annie spotted him and approached. He seemed to Annie quite like a frightened cat, nervous and jittery, though she supposed he could be shy around strangers.

"Mr. George, it's lovely to meet you finally," Annie beamed, trying to put the man at ease. "I hope you'll enjoy your stay here. Remind me again where you came from?"

Alexander's eyes darted around the room. "Kentucky," he replied, sniffing loudly. He pulled out a plain white handkerchief and blew his nose. "Allergies," he explained.

Annie gave him a sympathetic nod. "I'm the same every spring," she confided. "I should have bought stocks in Zyrtec," she laughed.

He stared at her for a moment. "I did," he replied finally, no hint of humor in his voice. When the conversation died there, Annie excused herself to greet another guest, a bubbly blonde woman who turned every head as she entered the room.

"Hi," she breathed, setting her bag down beside her feet. "I'm here to check in, is this the right place?" She looked around, wide-eyed and grinning. "Wow--it's so much prettier than the website pictures showed!"

Annie returned the blonde's smile. "I can check you in. Are you Kizzy?"

The blonde nodded. "Yes, ma'am. Kizzy Fitzsimmons, I booked a room online. I'm sorry I didn't get here earlier, but I had a little car trouble on the way up here."

"Where did you drive from?" Annie asked, motioning for Kizzy to enter the sitting room.

"Oh, just Myrtle Beach. I just finished a job there and decided to take a little time off before starting another one." Kizzy glanced at the other guests as she spoke, her eyes resting on Rob for a long moment. "I'm actually looking to move up this way," she added. "Myrtle Beach is getting way too crowded for my liking."

"Oh, that's funny," Annie replied, "There's a couple staying here that are also thinking of settling down here. Do you have any family around here?"

"No," Kizzy admitted. "I just got out of a bad relationship and really wanted to go someplace different. I saw your ad on the South Carolina tourism website and remembered visiting Coopersville when I was a little girl. It seemed like the universe was telling me something, so I booked a room right away." She blushed, "Also, you were one of the cheapest places to stay," she confessed.

"Well, you just happen to be one of our very first guests," Annie confided. The web ad had been Devon's idea, and so far the investment had paid off in spades. They were nearly fully booked for the next five weeks, and Annie was extremely relieved. "Let me get your room key and you can mingle with the other guests, if you like. We'll be serving snacks out on the back veranda shortly," she added.

"Cool." Kizzy made her way over to the window and pretended to appreciate the view, but Annie noticed that the only scenery Kizzy seemed truly interested in was Rob Reynolds. Sure enough, by the time Annie had returned with Kizzy's key, the pretty blonde and the handsome news anchor were deep in conversation.

Annie counted her guests silently, noting that two were still unaccounted for. She was about to turn and head back into her office to retrieve the booking list when a strange woman tapped her on the shoulder.

"Excuse me, but are you Annie Richards?" The woman was rail thin and very pale, as though she hadn't seen sunlight in her entire life. Her mousy brown hair frizzed out around her head like a muddy halo, except for on the top of her head where a sequined headscarf held it in place. Her eyes were too large for the rest of her face, giving her the appearance of a frightened animal. However, her voice was slow and soothing, somehow calm and airy all at the same time.

"I'm Annie. Are you--"

"Marie Robichaud, at your service." The woman smiled, which made her skin pull tight around her already-prominent cheek-bones. "I booked a room here for the week," she added, gesturing to her bags.

"Yes, Ms. Robichaud, it's a pleasure to meet you. Let me get you checked in and I'll get your room key." Annie took the woman's ID and headed back to the office for what felt like the hundredth time that day. She photocopied Marie's ID and added it to the others that she'd collected, then noted the woman's payment method and retrieved her room key. It amazed Annie how natural the whole process felt; it was as if she'd been running the place her entire life.

Annie grinned as she locked the office behind her and took Marie her room key. Once her guests had all deposited their belongings in their rooms, Annie invited them out to the back room for snacks and drinks. "In lieu of dinner, just for tonight, we've laid out a buffet of appetizers and drinks," she explained. "I just thought that this would be easier for everyone."

"Oh, that's perfect!" Kizzy cried, eyeing the table full of food. "Oh, and would you look--Annie's laid out wine and champagne! This is definitely the best bed-and-breakfast I've ever stayed at."

Annie blushed. "This isn't the typical spread," she confessed. "I just wanted something special for our very first guests. Now, I know that one of our guests indicated that he has food allergies, so I've made sure that we kept the shellfish and nuts well away from the other foods," she added. Everyone looked around, likely curious about who their allergic companion might be.

"There's also sweet tea and lemonade for those who don't drink alcohol," Bessie added, eyeing Mr. George. "Now, y'all enjoy yourselves and feel free to explore the property."

Rob and Chris appeared at Annie's side before she could wander off. "Annie, I was wondering if we could steal you away for just a few minutes before the sun starts to set," Rob began, pointing to his wrist as though he was wearing a watch. "Chris needs to get back to the station soon, and I'm ready to start my lovely stay here," he added. "I'd just love to get some video of you explaining the history of the plantation, if that's okay."

Annie's cheeks flushed red. "Oh, my, well, I guess I could. I mean, I'm not really dressed for an interview--"

Rob waved his hand in the air. "Oh, don't you worry one bit. You look lovely, and we'll only need a little footage, right Chris?"

The cameraman nodded, and Annie led the pair out the door of the screened-in veranda and down the gravel path to the wooden deck by the pond. She gave a brief rundown of the plantation's history, including its previous owners, or at least what she knew about them. "The house itself has some amazing charms," she told them. "Remind me to show you the hidden passageway in the kitchen and the hidden library in the sitting room," she added with a grin.

They paused long enough for Chris to capture some footage of the other guests on the screened in veranda. Marie watched them intently, managing to stay just out of sight of the camera, and Annie thought that she must be one of those kinds of people who were fascinated by cameras and publicity, but too shy to participate. After a few minutes, she led the men across the lawn and past the barn towards the little cemetery on the hill.

"This is one of my favorite parts of Rosewood Place," Annie explained, pointing out the graves that she and Rory had worked diligently to recover. "The Cooper family line pretty much died out here, and this little graveyard is all that's left of their family history, apart from a few recovered historical documents. Actually, remind me to show you Rose Cooper's diary when we go back to the house," she added.

"Rose Cooper? Which one was she?" Rob scanned the graves for names, but most were very hard to read.

"Here," Annie helped, pointing to a simple white stone that looked much newer than the rest. "I had her stone replaced since it was badly damaged. I figured that my guests might like to come out here and pay their respects once they've seen her diary."

"What's so special about Rose?"

Well, Annie thought, *for starters, she's buried with an absolute fortune in gold and jewels.* "Well, she died quite young, at the age of nineteen, and she died waiting for the love of her life to return from up north. It was quite sad, at least, I thought it was when I read about it in her diary. And of course, there's the fact that the plantation was named for her."

Rob seemed to be lost in thought for a moment, and when he came back to the present, he asked a question that made Annie uncomfortable, to say the least.

"Thomas Anderson and his niece Suzy were both murdered here on your property. Some people seem convinced that they were looking for some sort of long-lost treasure. Can you tell us everything that you know about that?"

3

Wining, Dining, And A Nosy Reporter

Annie narrowed her eyes and crossed her arms. "Did you really come here to interview me about my home's history or did you come here to poke a stick at a hornet's nest?" Annie had the sudden thought that she would be quite happy to lose Rob Reynolds as a customer if he was only going to go digging up the house's unfortunate past.

Rob raised one eyebrow. "Did I touch a nerve, Ms. Richards?"

Annie leaned forward, putting herself closer to Rob's face. "Thomas Anderson died a long time before I ever set foot on this property and Suzy Anderson was murdered by the same person who tried to kill me. So, yes, I'd say you have touched a nerve." She stared at him until he looked away. "I thought the rumors were quaint, but I can assure you that my decision to buy this place was based solely on my budget at the time, not on the off-chance that I might stumble across some hidden treasure." She took a step backward and Rob relaxed visibly. "I was horrified by Suzy's murder, and even more so when her killer came after me and my son. It was an awful experience, for sure, but I am doing my very best to put it behind me and move on."

Annie had been thrown right into the middle of a murder

investigation when her high school nemesis, Suzy Anderson, had wound up dead after threatening to take Rosewood Place from Annie. Hours after Suzy's death, Annie and Rory had stumbled across the long-dead remains of Suzy's uncle in the hay loft of the barn. The Andersons had been looking for the very treasure that lay hidden on her property. Annie swore that no good could possibly come from letting anyone else know about the plantation's buried secrets, and she just wanted the past to remain just that--*ancient history.*

She'd hoped that the media would leave her alone, but she knew that it was inevitable that a few die hard loonies would latch onto the story. She hadn't pegged Rob as a loony, but she supposed that it just proved that you never could tell."I know that must have been very difficult for you, since you knew the dead woman and all." Rob had obviously done his homework.

Annie sighed. "The whole sorry mess was covered in the newspapers, Mr. Reynolds. I don't really want to rehash all that. If you'd like to ask me more about the history of this place, that's fine, as long as it doesn't involve murders and crazy treasure hunters."

"So you really don't think that there's some sort of hidden treasure buried on the property?" Rob's eyes twinkled with curiosity. Annie softened slightly, recognizing the look as the same one Devon had when he first heard the stories of treasure hidden on Rosewood Place plantation.

"I wouldn't say that," she replied. "This house is a pretty spectacular treasure, wouldn't you agree? And the history of these people, the Coopers, is pretty valuable, at least to me." She hesitated. Annie knew that she couldn't ever tell the media the truth about the real treasure buried in Rose's grave. If she did, someone would insist on digging it up, and Annie couldn't stand the thought of Rose's grave being desecrated like that.

"There have been a few--very few--instances of people finding odd trinkets and treasures on the property. I found a very old coin here when I first moved in, and the Chief of Police found a similar one many years ago, so there is always the possibility that the past has left something behind for us." Annie smiled and gestured back towards the deck. "I think you've seen all the best parts of the property. You're welcome to film the inside of the house but I think I need to get back to the other guests. It looks like they've moved the socializing out on the deck by the pond if you'd care to join them."

Annie headed back towards the house with Rob and the cameraman following behind. She hoped that she'd nipped his curiosity in the bud, but reminded herself that human nature craved the unusual and morbid, so she might end up having to rehash the whole incident again at some point. For now, her explanation seemed to satisfy Rob. He led Chris on a short tour of the inside of the house before sending the cameraman off in the van.

"Will you need a ride when you check out?" Annie asked him.

"I'm sure I can get someone to come and pick me up," Rob replied. "But for now, I'm just going to enjoy your lovely home and hospitality." They stood by the table that held the appetizers and snacks. Annie shuffled empty dishes onto a tray while Rob picked at leftovers. "I'm sorry if I upset you up at the cemetery," he offered finally. "I'm really not that big of a jerk, but I just thought that if you had any insight into that whole murder-over-treasure mess, well, it might just help me get a lead story for once."

Annie picked up the tray and looked at Rob. He seemed sincere and slightly frustrated. She realized that he was probably a very good reporter stuck in a very boring job. After all, most journalists probably didn't dream of doing local reviews of small-town inns.

"Mr. Reynolds, I know you were just doing your job. And if I happen to find anything strange or unusual here on my property, how about I give you the first interview? I just hope you won't get your hopes up. No offense, but I wouldn't mind it one bit if I lived a very boring, uneventful life here until I grow old and die," she laughed.

Annie carried the tray full of dirty things into the kitchen while Rob piled a plate high with leftovers. He grabbed a glass of wine and made his way down to the deck where the other guests had congregated.

Eight wooden Adirondack-style chairs lined the deck and two large tables with sun parasols sat at one end, surrounded by sturdy wrought-iron patio chairs. The deck would easily hold twice as many people as its current number of occupants, and it had the perfect view of the setting sun beyond the murky green pond. Rory had designed it to be both a peaceful place to sip morning coffees and a fun spot for relaxing with a cold beer. Most of the guests seemed to be doing the latter, though Alexander George only nursed a lukewarm glass of lemonade.

Marie Robichaud sat at one of the tables, her rather large handbag perched beside her and a deck of tarot cards spread out in front of her. Kizzy listened intently as Marie read her fortune. From the look on Kizzy's face, she believed every word that the woman uttered.

"Do you see anything about my love life?" Kizzy asked, taking a large sip from her wine glass.

"Oh, yes," Marie purred, "I see a dark-haired stranger, a very handsome type who will try to sweep you off your feet."

Kizzy's eyes lit up. "That's much better than the cheating

blonde I left in Myrtle Beach," she replied, finishing off the wine in one gulp.

Frank and Doris each nursed a glass of champagne, and Frank looked as though he might just drift off to sleep at any moment. Rob settled in a chair across from them and smiled amiably. He pulled out his phone and was pleasantly surprised to find that the house's free WIFI reached the deck. He checked his social media while he sipped his own wine and nibbled the fried shrimp and cucumber sandwiches that he'd grabbed from the buffet.

It wasn't long before Doris announced that it was time for Frank and her to retire for the evening. "Goodnight, all! I guess we'll see you at breakfast in the morning," she added, patting Rob on the shoulder as she ambled past him.

A mosquito buzzed near his ear, and he swatted it absentmindedly. "It's the booze," Alexander said suddenly. "Mosquitoes are attracted to alcohol in your blood. That's why I'm sticking with lemonade," he added.

Rob was surprised that the man had spoken. He'd only heard him utter a handful of words since he'd arrived, and those had been sparse. "I guess I should have brought my bug spray," Rob replied.

"Citronella is effective usually," Alexander replied robotically. "We should suggest that our hostess put those candles out here to repel them." He fell silent and Rob struggled to keep the conversation going. Glancing around, he could see only Marie and Kizzy left, and he didn't want to be stuck chatting with the strange woman with her tarot cards. Kizzy seemed nice enough, but Marie gave him the creeps.

"Alexander, is it?" Mr. George nodded. "Do you mind if I ask what you do for a living?"

Alexander sniffed loudly. "I work at the post office." He offered no further explanation or detail, so Rob simply nodded.

"What brings you down to Coopersville?" Rob could see Kizzy heading back up the hill towards the house, and Marie was making a beeline for the chair next to him.

"I needed to get away for a bit." Alexander rubbed his eyes with the backs of his hands. "If you'll excuse me, I think it's past time I retired for the evening."

Rob checked his phone. It was a quarter to nine. "Okay, then, I guess I'll see you in the morning." Rob watched Alexander make his way up to the house. He tried to immerse himself in his phone, so he pulled up an ebook and pretended to read it.

"Those things are so antisocial, don't you think?" Marie sat down beside him, dropping her heavy bag on the deck with a loud thud. "I haven't properly introduced myself, I'm Marie Robichaud, spiritualist and psychic. Would you like to have your palm read?" She took a sip from her wine glass and smiled, displaying slightly crooked teeth with a leaf of what looked like spinach stuck between two of them.

Rob forced a smile. "Rob Reynolds, community news anchor." He shook her hand gently, then nodded to his phone. "Just catching up on some work, you know how it is."

Marie stared at him blankly. "Do you believe in fate, Mr. Reynolds?" She leaned in closer to him, peering into his eyes as though she was peering at a bug under a microscope.

Rob pulled back. "Uh, not really," he replied, preparing to get out of the chair.

"Hey, I brought a bottle!"

Rob and Marie both turned their heads at the same time to see Kizzy stumbling onto the deck in the near-dark. She carried an open bottle of wine that she grasped with both hands. "Oops-- nearly dropped it," she giggled.

Annie followed the young woman with a flashlight. "I'm so sorry, guys. These lights should have come on, but for some reason they haven't. I didn't want you all sitting here in the dark." She shone her flashlight along the railing of the deck at the back where several strands of lights were strung. A quick wave of her flashlight revealed the end of the lights and the plug, which should have been plugged into a small electrical outlet on one of the deck posts.

"Here," Rob offered, jumping out of his seat. "Let me help." He plugged the lights in while Annie held the flashlight, and the entire deck suddenly lit up with a gentle glow.

"That's better," Annie said loudly. Then, she whispered to Rob, "Keep an eye on Kizzy. That girl is going to have one heck of a hangover in the morning." She waved to the women, then headed back up to the veranda, her flashlight cutting a darting path as she walked.

Rob abandoned his chair and headed for one of the empty tables. Marie and Kizzy both followed him. *Great*, he thought, but he smiled the practiced greeting of a seasoned news anchor.

"So, Rob, what's it like being on television?" Kizzy poured herself another glass of wine and took a small sip. "You know, I've always wanted to be on TV."

Rob could feel his cheeks glowing in the low light. He hated being asked about his job. It wasn't that he was ashamed of covering community events, he just imagined that he'd be doing more hard-hitting stories four years into his career at the local news station. "Oh, it's not that big of a deal, really, " he replied.

"You are very modest, I can tell that about you," Marie intoned. "Your aura is practically buzzing--it's very powerful," she cooed. She reached into her purse and pulled out a small pot of what looked like lip balm. She opened it up and applied it liberally to her lips, then offered the pot to Kizzy, who declined the offer.

"What's my aura like?" Kizzy asked, the last two words running together slightly.

Marie cocked her head to one side and squinted. "It's a little green right now, dear. I think you'd better lay off the wine a little bit."

Kizzy hiccuped slightly, then pushed her glass away. "Oh, maybe you're right. I don't usually drink like this," she apologized, "but I've had such a crappy week. First I lost my job at the dinner theater down in Myrtle Beach, and then my ex comes blowing back into town, looking for money from me. Talk about a mess--I must seem such a loser to you two."

Marie didn't answer but patted Kizzy's arm in solidarity. "Well, you can't win them all." She glanced from Kizzy to Rob, then puckered her lips as though she'd tasted something bitter. "If you'll excuse me, I believe I heard Annie say something about a library. I do believe I'll go pick something out for some bedtime reading."

She didn't wait for a response, but sashayed off into the thickening darkness with her heavy purse slung over her shoulder. "Boy, everyone else seems to be real early birds, don't you think? I usually never go to bed before midnight," admitted Kizzy.

"Yeah, I guess we're just night owls," grinned Rob. He glanced at his phone. "It's not even nine-thirty," he added, stifling a yawn.

Kizzy laughed out loud at him and he blushed again. "Well, I would be a night owl if my job didn't have me up so stinking early every day," he chuckled. They made small talk, discussing the house and the other guests, then fell into a companionable silence until Kizzy suggested that maybe they should go to bed.

"Alone," she clarified.

"I wouldn't have suggested anything else," Rob flirted. They made their way back up to the veranda. Rob held the door for Kizzy, but the peaceful silence of the evening was interrupted by a loud dance tune. Kizzy jumped, then pulled her cell phone from her back pocket.

"Oh, crap." She touched the screen and rejected the call.

"What's up?" Rob still stood with the door wide open and he suddenly felt like he could sleep for days.

The phone in Kizzy's hand sprang to life once again. "It's my ex. I guess I need to answer this--I left him on sort of bad terms."

Rob cocked a sleepy eyebrow. "What kind of bad?"

Kizzy gritted her pearly white teeth. "I kind of stole his car," she confided. "It's a long story, and I'll tell you all about it tomorrow, but for now, I need to talk to him, or he won't stop calling me." She apologized again even as she answered the call, and Rob watched as she strolled back down to the wooden deck to have some privacy. With a sigh, he stepped into the screened in room and made his way into the house and upstairs to his waiting bed.

4

More Permanent Quarters

Annie felt bad about leaving her guests in the dark out by the pond, but fortunately, she'd discovered her lighting problem before anyone fell and injured themselves. She'd only noticed the problem while clearing up the last of the dishes from the veranda, and once she'd rectified the situation, and made sure that Kizzy didn't break her neck trying to liberate the last bottle of wine, she sent her mother off to bed and joined Devon and Rory on the front porch.

"All good out there?" Rory asked, grinning as he took one of Devon's chess pieces from the giant board they were playing on.

"All good," she replied, dropping into an oversized rocking chair with a sigh. She was pleased that none of her guests had decided to hang out here on the front porch. At least for now it still felt like a refuge for her and her family. She watched as her son struggled to choose a move that wouldn't put his queen in check.

"You are not beating me again, old man," Devon cried, moving his knight with a flourish to put Rory's own queen in jeopardy. "So, Mom, I hear we're going to be famous," Devon said, pushing himself back from the table. Annie gave him a puzzled look. "You know, that news guy? I bet we get tons of business after he puts that video on the air."

Annie shrugged her shoulders. "I guess we'll see," she replied. "I'm not too worried about it, though. The internet ad seems to be working really well. Now I just need to make sure my guests don't break a leg and sue me before the business really takes off." She explained about the lights and how she'd had to play superhero by going down to the deck and plugging them back in.

Rory, listened, then shook Devon's hand, ending the game in a gentlemanly spirit. He leaned back in his chair and put his hands behind his neck. "I'll try and rig up something a little more permanent for the deck," he said thoughtfully. "Though, to be fair, I don't see how those lights came unplugged. Once you plug them in, they're pretty secure."

Devon cleared his throat. "Uh, well, that might be my fault," he replied sheepishly. "I sort of charged my phone down on the deck while I was helping Rory paint the chairs. I guess I forgot to plug the lights back in."

"Well, there you go," offered Rory. "No harm done, and I'm sure Devon will remember to plug them in next time."

Annie felt a little better about the whole situation, but there was another problem that gnawed at her. "One of the guests didn't turn up," she said suddenly. "Mr. Ross. I tried to call him a couple of times but it went straight to his voicemail."

"Maybe he just got delayed, stuck in traffic or something," Devon suggested. "Mom, seriously, you worry way too much."

Rory nodded in agreement. "I wouldn't worry. Give it until tomorrow, then if he doesn't show up, you can try again. Did he book for more than a few days?"

"He booked an entire week. I took down his credit card

information but he said he'd prefer to pay cash. He sounded like a nice enough guy when I spoke to him on the telephone," she added. "There was this one weird thing, though. He asked if he could have a package delivered here. He said it was a gift for his mother in Mobile and since he wouldn't be home to accept it, he asked if he could have it sent here."

Rory thought about this for a moment. "You're right, that is weird. Devon's probably right, though. He probably just got held up somewhere. I wouldn't be surprised if he turns up in the middle of the night, banging on the door, crying about car trouble or something like that."

"Maybe you're right. Besides, it's not like there's anything I can do about it. If he doesn't show up I've still got his deposit. And if a package arrives, well, I guess I'll deal with that if it actually happens."

"See, problem solved," replied Rory.

"I guess I'm just a little stressed having all these people here at once," Annie confessed. "I know I'll get used to it, but right now I'm just thinking of all the things that could go wrong."

"Mom, you've got this. We've got this," he added. "It's going to be totally cool, as long as that crazy fortune-teller lady doesn't try to read my palm," he added. "She seems like a real nutcase."

Annie grinned. "Well, I did promise that you'd meet some unusual characters living in a country inn. Just think--you'll be able to write an essay all about it when you head back to school in a few weeks."

Devon groaned. "Way to ruin my good mood, Mother. On that note, I think I'll go upstairs to my *private* room and watch some Netflix." He stood, stretched, and stooped to give his mother a peck on the cheek before he headed into the house, pausing long enough to say goodnight to his mother and Rory.

"He's a good kid, Annie." Rory began packing the chess pieces away in their storage box. "He's going to be fine. The high school is probably a lot smaller than he's used to, but it's bigger than this place," he grinned. "And at least the people there are his age. I would have gone crazy spending so much time with my parents when I was his age."

"I know, I know. It's just--I worry that he won't make friends. I worry that he'll get singled out because he's not from around here."

"I'd worry about the girls following him home," Rory teased. "That boy's a born charmer and he's from the Big City. The girls will love that. I think we might have to get that barn fixed up pretty quick just in case there's a wedding in your near future," he teased.

"Oh, no. He's not getting married until he's at least thirty," she joked. "And I think I have a better project for you to focus on than the barn, at least for now."

Rory cocked his head to one side. "Oh, yeah? What's that? Does your mama want a bigger chicken coop?"

"Oh, no, you don't," she laughed. "She's got all the chickens that she's allowed to have. I'm not turning this place into a poultry farm."

"Hey, they keep the bug population down," he argued. "But, yeah, they can stink a little," he relented.

"I think you should build a cabin."

"Like a log cabin?" Rory scratched the back of his head. "I'm not sure that I know how."

"It doesn't have to be a log cabin, just a small bungalow or something."

"You know, I'd thought about that. I saw an inn up in the mountains that offered bungalows as well as rooms. I think that would be perfect for families, especially if we put in a little kitchenette in each one."

"No, that's not what I meant," Annie clarified. "I mean a place for you. It would be like a handyman's cabin. Or bungalow-- whatever you want to call it."

"But, I'm fine in my camper," Rory replied.

"Yeah, but Rory, it's a camper. I mean, it can't be as comfortable as your own little house, can it?" She struggled to find a way to put her next sentence that wouldn't sound offensive. "And besides, I'm not sure the camper really fits the overall look of the place." Rory's face tensed. "Oh, god, that came out wrong. I'm not saying that your camper is ugly. It's an awesome camper, but I'd like a more permanent place for you to stay."

"Are you asking me to live here forever?" Rory's eyebrow shot up, and his lips twitched. "Is that your way of tying me down after all these years?"

Annie's cheeks blushed in the glow of the porch light. "No, Rory Jenkins, I am not trying to tie you down. I just thought that our live-in handyman ought to have a place to live in."

Rory laughed. "I know what you meant, woman. And I appreciate the idea. I'd be happy to build it for you and I'll even live in it, if you want me to. I can store the camper at my parents' place. My mother won't mind," he added.

Annie felt relieved that Rory hadn't taken offense at her suggestion. She'd been so relieved to find that their relationship had somehow managed to slip into a familiar rhythm despite their romantic history. They had developed an easy friendship that felt natural and *good*. Occasionally a memory from their past would catch her off-guard, and the thought of what might have been tried to sneak its way into her mind, but she was careful to cut those thoughts out before they had a chance to take root.

She was often surprised by how little she missed her late husband, David. His death had ultimately seemed anticlimactic to her, as though she'd already mourned his loss throughout their marriage. She supposed that she'd actually mourned the marriage itself long before she found out that her husband had been cheating on her, which no doubt lessened the blow of his death.

Rory wasn't a substitute for David, but he was many of the things that David wasn't for her. He was a good friend, he was reliable, and he made her laugh. He loved her mother and her son and he seemed to fit well with her little family. While a tiny part of her wondered whether they would stand a chance if they tried to pick up where their romantic relationship had ended all those years ago, a larger part of her was scared that it would disrupt this perfect, delicate balance that they'd struck as friends.

"I'm really glad that you're here, Rory," Annie said quietly. "I appreciate all that you've done for us more than you could ever know."

Rory smiled back at her. "I appreciate you, too, Annie Purdy." She'd become used to him using her maiden name. After all, it's what he'd called her all those years ago. "I reckon it's time for me to hit the sack. I've got a busy day tomorrow, and by the look of a few of your guests, I'm guessing you will, too."

They rose from their chairs and said their goodnights. Annie watched as Rory made his way down the steps of the front porch and out into the darkness towards his camper. Then she pulled the front door closed behind her, locked it out of habit, and headed upstairs to her own room, hoping that a peaceful night's sleep would lead to a busy, but otherwise uneventful week. Unfortunately for Annie, things wouldn't work out quite that way.

5

A Missing Guest Is Found

Annie had learned long ago that she had to get up very early to beat Bessie Purdy at rising. Bessie was literally up with the chickens, often waking at five in the morning to prepare coffee, feed her birds, and sneak Devon's cat, TigerLily, a few extra treats before the rest of the house woke.

Annie's mother was one of those lucky souls who seemed to require less sleep than most other human beings. She wandered off to bed after ten on most nights, sometimes reading in bed for hours before giving in to sleep. Annie needed more sleep than she ever seemed to get, but on the first morning of her fully-booked inn's grand opening, she was up right behind her mother, her nerves still jangling in anticipation of the house's first full day as a guest house.

Annie dressed quickly and headed straight to the kitchen, following her nose to find her mother patiently tending to the coffeemaker. She grinned as her mother tried to hide the fact that she was feeding the young orange cat cream straight from the fridge. "You'll give that cat an upset stomach," she teased before pouring cream into her own mug of coffee.

"Nonsense. Farm cats drink milk straight from the cow," she

added. "TigerLily could be a proper farm cat if we had a proper cow," Bessie sniffed.

"It is too early to argue with you about cows, Mother." Annie stirred her coffee and looked out the window. The sun was beginning to rise and her guests would be looking for their own cups of coffee soon. "Why don't we go sit on the deck and drink these?" she asked. "It's going to be a beautiful, hot day soon--let's go sit out by the water before it gets too hot."

Bessie grinned. "That's the best part about living here," she sighed. "It's like having our own little bit of paradise this early in the morning." They left the house through the door in the kitchen rather than cutting through the rest of the house. It would be quieter this way and mean that they'd be less likely to wake the sleeping guests.

Annie was happy to see that the lights were still on around the deck. She realized that leaving them on all day would be impractical, but since they were LED lights, she wasn't overly worried about how much energy they used. She made a mental note to have Rory look online for some solar-powered ones later, debated with herself over whether their cost would be worth it, then resigned herself to the fact that worry-free lights were less expensive than a lawsuit from someone tripping on a darkened deck.

Bessie and Annie sat at one of the tables near the back of the deck and sipped their coffee in silence for a few minutes. Annie stared out across the pond, watching the tiny ripples where water bugs landed bravely, wary of the fish, turtles, and other creatures that lurked beneath the murky water. The sunlight glistened along one edge of the pond, sending shimmers of gold and rose out across the surface of the water.

Living in New York, Annie had missed being so close to nature.

She'd spent many hours in Central Park, but it wasn't the same. Even on a quiet day in the Park she could still feel the presence of the City looming over her. Here, there was nothing. Her closest neighbor was several miles away. She could barely see the road from her driveway, and there was no roar of traffic or chatter of people, just the sound of insects and birds waking up around her.

"Beautiful, isn't it?" Bessie said quietly. "I used to love drinking coffee outside with your dad before he passed. He'd probably be fishing right now if he was still alive," she added, blinking back an errant tear.

Annie nodded. She missed her father more on days like this, when the world felt brand new and sleepy all at the same time. She liked to think that he was watching her sometimes, approving of how much she'd overcome and how hard she'd worked to help bring the plantation and its house back to life.

As she stared out across the pond, a redbird fluttered into sight and landed on one of the deck posts. "Oh," Bessie whispered. "Would you look at that!"

Annie didn't know much about birds but she thought that it might be a cardinal. It was a deep shade of red that stood out against the green and brown of the treeline behind it. It seemed to Annie that the bird was watching her and her mother, waiting for an invitation.

"You know what they say about red birds visiting you, don't you?" Bessie smiled.

"No, what do they say?"

"That it's the spirit of a loved one, come to visit you." Bessie sighed. "That's your father, I'm sure of it."

Annie watched the bird hop from foot to foot, peering down at the water below it. It was a lovely superstition, and part of her wanted it to be true, but it was a little disconcerting to think of her father flying around and watching her from a bird's body. Before she could reply to her mother's cryptic comment, the bird flew away, disappearing into the woods on the other side of the pond.

A glint of metal caught Annie's eye as the bird departed. She looked down at the deck below where the bird had been perched and saw a cell phone lying on the edge of the deck.

"Well, now, that's lucky," she mumbled, rising from her seat. She walked over and picked up the phone. "Someone left their phone out here," she called to her mother. "They're lucky it didn't go in the pond during the night."

Annie noticed that the phone's screen was locked and required a password to unlock it. "I guess I'll just take this inside and ask around. Someone will be missing it, I imagine." As she turned to walk back to her mother, something in the water caught her eye. She leaned over the edge of the deck, trying to get a better look.

"What is it?" Bessie asked, already making her own way to where Annie stood.

Annie didn't answer. She didn't have to. Bessie's gasp matched her own, and both women stepped back from the edge of the deck as though the thing in the water might just rise up and bite them.

"Is that--is he--"

"Dead? I think so," Annie finished her mother's question.

"Who is it?" Bessie asked, putting a hand to her mouth.

"I can't tell," Annie replied, peering over the edge once more. "Do you think it's one of the guests?"

Bessie shook her head. "I don't know, but I know how we can find out." She knelt down by the edge of the deck.

"Mother! You are not touching that body!" Annie's voice was

39

louder than she'd intended.

"You're right--I might contaminate the crime scene," Bessie conceded, rising to her feet.

"How do you know it's a crime scene? He could have just fallen in and drowned," Annie said, hoping that this was the case, yet praying that it wasn't. An accidental drowning could mean the kiss of death for her business, but a murder could be even worse.

"Let's go inside and give Emmett a call," Bessie suggested. "He'll know what to do. And we can do a headcount to see if anyone is missing," she added.

Annie didn't like the idea of leaving the body unattended in the pond, but she knew her mother's plan was the best one. She glared at the cell phone in her hand, hoping that she hadn't just contaminated a piece of evidence, like her mother suggested. Grabbing her coffee cup from the table, Annie squared her shoulders and headed for the house. It was going to be a long day, and she was definitely going to need another cup of coffee.

6

Questions, Alibis, and Answers

Emmett Barnes loved visiting Rosewood Place. He enjoyed fishing in its quiet pond on lazy Sundays. Food served at Bessie Purdy's dinner table always seemed to taste better, and he'd taken a shine to the little family that had transformed the rundown farmhouse into a spectacular bed-and-breakfast. Emmett would have been happy to come out to the old farm for a visit at any time, but the reason for today's visit was definitely one that he could do without.

He watched as Alan Sherman from the fire department hauled the soggy body out of his beloved fishing hole. "Oh, yeah, he's dead." The fireman's statement was blunt and unnecessary. Unless blue skin was an indicator of perfect health, it was pretty clear that the person who had just been floating in the pond was a goner.

Emmett watched the paramedics load the strange man's body onto a stretcher and prepare to take it to the county morgue. He sighed at the thought of all the paperwork his visit would elicit, and he groaned as he realized that he'd have to spend the morning supervising the inquiry into the man's death. For some reason, Delbert Plemmons had insisted on coming out to help with the inquiry. Delbert had been a police officer for almost three years but he seemed to approach every investigation as though it was his first. Delbert loved being a police officer, but Emmett couldn't help but think that the job didn't quite love Delbert the same way.

"Chief," Delbert called out, averting his eyes from the body as it was carried past him. "Would you like me to start interviewing the guests that are staying here?"

Emmett twisted one side of his bushy mustache. "How many are there?"

Delbert pulled a small notebook out of his breast pocket. "Uh, lemme see--there's six guests checked in and then there's Annie--Mrs. Richards," he corrected himself, "and her mama and son. And the handyman," he added, curling his lips around the word like as if it tasted of something bitter.

Emmett knew that Delbert was mildly infatuated with Annie Richards. Though Delbert was much younger than Annie, he seemed smitten with her all the same, blushing frequently when he spoke to her, finding excuses to accompany Emmett to the old plantation when he visited. Emmett knew that the infatuation was strictly one-way, Annie had no interest in Delbert whatsoever, but he saw no reason to say anything to the young officer. His fascination was likely to fade soon enough, and as long as it didn't cloud his investigative skills, Delbert could continue to worship Annie from afar.

Emmett glanced at Delbert's list of guests. "Why don't you go talk to Miss Fitzsimmons, Miss Robichaud, and Mr. George. I'll talk to Mr. Reynolds and the Martins, then I'll chat with Annie and see what she and her mama can tell me."

If Delbert was disappointed in not being asked to speak to Annie he hid it well, blushing as he interviewed Kizzy.

Delbert's pale cheeks were remarkably pink as he wrote down her movements the previous night.

"So you were the last person out here on the deck," Delbert asked after hearing Kizzy explain how she'd taken a private phone call after Rob had gone back inside the house.

"Yes, but I swear I didn't see anybody else out here. I mean, I would have heard somebody falling in the water, I wasn't that drunk." It was Kizzy's turn to blush. "What I meant to say was that even though I had a few drinks, I was not out of my mind. My phone call sort of sobered me up," she added.

"Who were you talking to?"

"My ex. We were actually arguing, sort of. Well, he was yelling at me, and I was doing my best not to listen. You see, back when we were dating, I bought him a car so he could drive to work. He was supposed to make payments on it, but he lost his job. We broke up a few weeks ago, but he refused to pay me for the car and he wouldn't just give it back, so I sort of liberated it from his place and hit the road." She waited for Delbert to say something, but he just nodded. "But the loan was in my name, too. I've been making the payments so my credit wouldn't get wrecked, so it's mine, right?"

"Uh, I reckon--I uh, yeah." He made a few more notes in his notepad. "We're probably going to need to see your phone to corroborate your story," he replied almost apologetically.

Kizzy's face fell. "Oh, that's going to be a problem. I can't find it. I was so sure that I put it on the table beside my bed, but when I woke up, I couldn't find it."

"Exactly how much did you drink last night?" Kizzy's glare shrunk Delbert just a little. "Do you think the phone was stolen?" Delbert asked, changing the subject quickly.

"I don't see how," Kizzy admitted. "I mean, my bedroom door

was shut and locked all night."

Delbert suddenly had an idea. "What does your phone look like?"

Kizzy described her phone, and Delbert nodded his head. "I think I know where it is." He asked Kizzy to wait while he approached the Chief, who had finished interviewing the Martins and was now talking to the news anchor.

After a brief chat with Delbert, Emmett left Rob and approached Kizzy. "Miss Fitzsimmons, I'm Emmett Barnes, the Chief of Police. I believe that we have found your phone," he said, holding up an evidence bag that held the phone that Annie found. "But I'm afraid we're going to have to hold onto it for a little bit. Once the fellas down at the lab look it over and can corroborate your statement, we'll get it right back to you."

Kizzy nodded slowly and sat down on the steps of the veranda. Rob joined her while Delbert and Emmett finished interviewing the guests. After statements were taken and questions answered, the guests were allowed to return to their rooms. Annie, Bessie, Rory, and Emmett stood on the deck overlooking the pond. Emmett had promised them answers, at least as much as he knew already. It would be a few days before some of their questions could be answered, but he filled them in on what he knew.

"According to the man's driver's license, his name is Lou Ross. I believe he's your missing guest, Annie."

"He was supposed to check in yesterday," Annie confirmed.

"We found his car parked out back with the others. I'm guessing that he pulled up through the grass and not the gravel," he added, "or you might have heard him come in."

"But why would he come sneaking in here in the middle of the night? It doesn't make any sense," Bessie lamented.

"I'm not sure, Bessie. Maybe he was drunk, maybe he was trying to be polite and not wake everyone up--whatever the reason, we'll figure it out." He paused for a moment. "Are you sure none of the other guests knew Mr. Ross? Nobody was expecting him?"

Annie shook her head. "No, just Mama, Rory, and myself." She explained about the man's request to have a package delivered to the farmhouse, and Emmett frowned.

"Have you received any packages yet?"

"No, but do you think that could have something to do with his death?" There was something sad and disturbing about a package being delivered to someone after their death that sent a shiver down Annie's spine.

"I'm not sure," Emmett replied, "but I do know that somebody ransacked Mr. Ross' car pretty thoroughly last night. He had a couple of suitcases in there that had been emptied out everywhere. One of the windows was smashed in, too."

Annie felt sick to her stomach. Someone had driven onto her property, vandalized a guest's car, and a guest had drowned in her pond, all while she slept soundly in her bed. "Oh, Emmett, do you think I should close the house and send all the guests away? I mean, is there a chance that my guests are in danger?"

"Hold on, Annie," Rory interjected. "First of all, we don't know if the guy in the pond was murdered or if he just had too much to drink and fell into the water. For all we know he could have vandalized his own car. You're blaming yourself for something you had no control over, so don't punish your business or your guests by jumping to conclusions."

Emmett nodded. "Rory's right. If your guests want to stay, I see no reason why they shouldn't. It's sad, but accidents do happen," he added. "You might want to have some sort of security system put in place out here, though. Maybe get some of those motion-activated lights or some security cameras to point out over your guests' cars. That way if anything else does happen you'll be able to see it."

"Excuse me, Chief." No one heard Rob approach. Annie actually jumped at the sound of his voice. For a moment she'd forgotten that she had a house full of confused people waiting for her to make some sort of statement about their safety. "Could I ask you a few questions?"

Emmett eyed Rob warily. "Off the record?" Emmett had known Rob for a long time, and he trusted the news reporter's ethics. However, the circumstances around the drowned man in Annie's pond weren't sitting right with the seasoned police officer, and he didn't want to get reporters involved until he knew more about the whole situation.

"Well, no, actually." Rob stepped onto the deck. "Look, I know that the last thing you want is the press to come swooping in here and causing a scene. I believe you when you said that the death was likely an accident, but I don't think the guy was alone. I don't want Annie being overrun with insensitive newshounds," he said, nodding in her direction. "What if you give me an exclusive interview about the man's tragic death and then keep me posted if things develop. I'll be staying here all week anyway, regardless of how your investigation turns out."

It sounded to Annie like Rob had rehearsed his speech before approaching Emmett. She was relieved that at least one guest wanted to stay, although the fact that said guest was a news reporter left her feeling a little antsy.

"Look," he added, his confident tone slipping into more of a plea. "This could be the perfect opportunity for me to cover something more hard-hitting than the local bake sales and business openings, no offense intended. This is real news, and I want to show my bosses that I can be a real news reporter." He seemed to Annie a bit like a puppy that was begging for a bone, all earnest eyes and careful anticipation of her reply.

"Rob, I'm happy that you want to stay, but I'm not sure if you should even be covering this--event." She frowned. "Though, I suppose that the newspaper or news station will just send someone else anyway."

Emmett nodded. "Annie, if you're going to talk to a reporter, you might as well talk to Rob here. But I wouldn't talk to anyone else. You don't need any more negative publicity surrounding this place." He glanced up towards the house. "Don't make any statements, official or otherwise, until I get the coroner's report. And don't talk to the other guests about the whole thing," he said, directing the last command at both Annie and Rob. "I don't know those other folks. I don't know what their motives are or if they're telling me the truth."

Rob nodded immediately. "You have my word, Emmett. I won't say a thing until you give me the go-ahead, and I'll try to make sure that what I report doesn't have any negative impact on Annie's business."

"If it had been anybody else but you, Rob..." he trailed off. "And I meant what I said about being cautious. Don't speak to anyone that isn't directly involved in this investigation, Annie. Even an accidental drowning can ruin a business. I really don't want to see this place fail before it's even had a chance to get off the ground."

Annie let out a long sigh. Neither did she, but as long as she kept finding dead bodies on her property, Annie wasn't too sure that her business could possibly stay alive.

7

Business, As Usual

After Emmett and his crew had finally cleared up and left, Annie marched herself back up to the house feeling defeated but not quite broken.

"Maybe people will still want to stay," Rob suggested, trying to lift her spirits. "I mean, it's like Emmett said, accidents happen all the time. It's no reason for the other guests to cut short a whole vacation, right?"

Annie appreciated Rob's efforts to make her feel better, but she really couldn't blame her guests if they wanted to leave. She supposed that she should be glad that no one had actually known the dead man. If the others had actually met him and spoken with him they would likely be much more distraught than they were now.

As Annie entered the sitting room, she realized that her guests were much less distressed than she'd expected them to be. Raucous laughter filled the room and she could see Frank, Doris, and Kizzy crowded around her iPad. Devon grinned at her from across the room.

"Mom, Grandma Bessie, you've got to come see this video. It's hilarious!"

The room went silent for a moment as the others realized that Annie had returned. Annie glimpsed the screen of the iPad in time to see the last few seconds of a compilation video featuring clips of babies and cats. "I thought it might lighten the mood a little," Devon explained sheepishly.

Annie smiled at him. "That's a wonderful idea. It's been a tough morning," she added. "I'm so sorry about everything," she continued, addressing her guests. Her stomach rumbled. The iPad's clock showed that it was nearly noon. "Oh, I'm so sorry--you all are probably starving!" They'd missed breakfast while the police had been questioning everyone. "Give me a few minutes and we'll whip up something for lunch." She turned to her mother, eyes wide with panic.

"Oh, no, dear. Doris and I took care of that already, didn't we, Doris?" Bessie smiled brightly as Doris nodded.

"When did you have time to come in here and cook?" Annie was relieved and confused all at once, and she was a little jealous that everyone else had eaten. Her stomach growled again, much to her embarrassment.

"Oh, it was just instant oatmeal," Bessie explained. "Doris and I had a lovely time, didn't we?"

Doris grinned. "Your mother is such a hoot! Oh, and that kitchen--I told Frank he'd better make sure our house has one just like it when we retire down here," she laughed.

"Well, thank goodness for you, Mama," Annie sighed. "I'm sorry everyone. I feel like I've let you all down somehow."

"What do you mean?" Kizzy slouched into the corner of the sofa and rubbed her eyes with the backs of her hands. "It's not your fault some dummy decided to go drown himself in your pond."

Everyone stared at Kizzy. She blushed. "I mean, it was a

horrible accident, but it's definitely not your fault. And I never eat breakfast anyway," she added.

Annie forced a weak smile. "Thank you, Kizzy, but I completely understand if the events this morning have made any of you want to rethink your stay here." She made herself look up and into the eyes of everyone in the room. "I'm prepared to refund your deposits, if you want to leave."

The response from the room wasn't what she expected. Kizzy looked like she might cry, Doris laughed, and Marie Robichaud simply snorted. Mr. George was the only person who reacted the way Annie had expected him to. He simply blew his nose and shrugged his shoulders, an offering of quiet indifference that told her absolutely nothing about what he was thinking.

"I'm not going anywhere," Frank said quickly. "That drive down here almost killed me," he complained. "Try spending over ten hours in a car listening to chick novels on audiobook, see how you like it. No, thank you. We'll just take our chances here, Mrs. Richards." He glanced at his wife and leaned towards Annie. "At least if I drown, I won't have to listen to those darned audio books anymore," he joked.

"I don't want to leave," Kizzy offered. "I don't really have any plans after I leave here. I sort of thought I might use this week to figure some things out."

Marie looked around. "Well, if everyone else is staying, I may as well stay, too. After all, it is my vacation," she cooed. "And of course, I don't mind dead people one bit. In fact, I talk to them all the time." She said this without a trace of humor, but Devon couldn't help chuckling. Marie glared at him. "What? You don't believe me? I make a living with my spiritual abilities, young man. Ghosts and spirits are no laughing matter."

"Well, I think we're all agreed that nobody has to go anywhere,"

Doris offered, "so if you don't mind, I'd love a cup of hot tea and some more of those cookies Bessie was handing out yesterday, if you have them."

Something loosened in Annie's chest and she felt as though she'd been granted some sort of stay of execution. No one wanted to leave. She wouldn't be refunding everyone's money and shutting the doors behind them. Rosewood Place lived to fight again--but only if she kept everyone happy. And safe.

"I'll bring them right out," Bessie replied, scurrying off to the kitchen with Annie following right behind. The two women grabbed each other by the arms once they were out of earshot of the guests. "I don't know how you did that," Bessie began, "but you just saved our bacon."

Annie shook her head. "I didn't do anything," she insisted. "They just like us. I mean, they really like us." Annie busied herself with preparing sandwiches while Bessie loaded a tray with cookies, creamer, sugar, and tea bags. Ten minutes later the sitting room was abuzz with the chatter of Annie's guests.

Devon excused himself, liberating his mother's iPad from Mr. George and a handful each of cookies and sandwiches from Bessie. Annie noticed that Rory had slipped away while she was in the kitchen. She got the distinct impression that being around so many people was a little taxing on him. Of course, the fact that he'd spent several years in prison didn't help his social claustrophobia. His unfortunate past behind him, Annie was well aware of how difficult it was for Rory to be in a room filled with strangers.

Rob and Kizzy were deep in conversation, discussing Coopersville and the job prospects. Kizzy seemed to have tamed her flirting considerably since the night before, the lack of alcohol leaving her a slightly restrained, though no less bubbly, version of herself. Annie liked the girl, though she feared that Kizzy might be one of those young women who made terrible choices and who always seemed to find themselves in the middle of a whirlwind of drama.

"You know," Rob said, loud enough to include Annie in the conversation, "I used to wonder about this place. When I was a kid we'd drive past here and my parents would comment about what a shame it was that this old house was so run-down. It kind of had a reputation, you know."

"As what?" Annie was delighted to hear someone speak of the house's past. She was happy to soak up every detail of its history, no matter how small or how recent.

"Oh, all the kids said it was haunted," he replied. "It sure looked haunted to me. But now--" he looked around the room with admiration, "now it looks amazing. Who did you hire to do the renovations? These antebellum houses can be a nightmare to restore."

"Oh, there was just the one contractor," Annie replied. "Rory did it. Well, he did most of it. I picked out paint colors and furniture and got in his way--a lot," she added with a chuckle. "He's a huge history buff, so he already knew what it should look like, more or less."

"It sure is beautiful," Kizzy agreed. "I used to dream of living in a big old house like this," she added. "It's like something out of an old movie, isn't it?" Annie agreed. "So, are you and Rory like, a couple, or something?"

Annie felt her cheeks flush slightly. No matter how many times she explained her relationship with Rory, it always felt awkward. "We're just friends," she said finally. "Very old friends. I knew him in high school, and when I came back into town he was kind enough to take on the renovation work for me when I couldn't

52

find anyone else to help."

"That's a great friend," Rob noted with a smile. "And he stayed around after the work was done--that's a great contractor." He lowered his voice and leaned towards Annie. "You know, the house isn't the only one with a lot of history. Rory--"

"I'm aware of Rory's history," Annie cut him off. "And that's exactly what it is: ancient history." She smiled, sensing that Rob's intentions were good, but nipping that line of conversation in the bud just the same. "Rory had an unfortunate incident in his past, but he paid his debt. Now, can I get you two any more tea?"

Kizzy looked a little confused but thankfully didn't ask any questions. When she excused herself to visit the restroom, Rob sidled up to Annie. "I apologize if my question came across the wrong way. It's just, well, you seem like a very nice lady. I don't really know Rory, but I knew of his history. If you say he's a decent guy, I believe it."

Annie laughed. "You don't have to believe me. Spend an hour with the guy--he's smart, funny, and extremely kind. He just made a mistake, like I'm sure we all have at some point in time." Rory had gotten into a bar fight that left his attacker in critical condition. Annie had married a man who largely ignored her and their son while he cheated on her. Sometimes she thought her mistake had been a much larger one than Rory's, although her prison had been a figurative one only.

"I really admire you, Annie." Rob's admission caught Annie by surprise. "I know a little about your history," he confessed, "about your husband's death and why you came back to South Carolina. That really took a lot of bravery."

Well, someone's done their research. Annie shook her head. "I wasn't being brave; I was being practical. My financial situation wasn't working out for me in New York, so I decided to come back here and take on a big old wreck of a house, turn it into a really classy inn, and invite people to come find dead bodies in my pond," she quipped. "I'd say it's working out pretty well, so far."

By the time Kizzy returned from the restroom, Annie was ready for a break from entertaining her houseguests. She excused herself, leaving Bessie and Doris chatting away in one corner of the room while Frank snoozed in his chair, a crumb of sandwich stuck in his gray beard, and Marie sitting in the other corner of the room, her tarot cards spread out before her.

Rob and Kizzy opted to take a stroll around the property to work up an appetite before dinner. Annie had no idea where Mr. George had wandered off to, but since he complained so often of his allergies, she doubted that she'd find him wandering around outside, at mercy to the pollen and allergens of the Great Outdoors.

Stepping out onto the house's large front porch, Annie was greeted by the sound of hammering and laughter. She followed her ears to the barn, where Devon and Rory were working on what looked like a piece of railing. Their noise stopped when they noticed her, but she protested. "Don't stop on my account. You two sounded like you were having a great time," she added with a grin.

Rory gestured towards the railing. "I just thought maybe I'd add this to the end of the deck. I know you wanted to leave it open so the view of the pond was unobscured, but I sort of thought this would cover you in case anyone else decides to get a little tipsy down by the pond."

Annie sighed. "You're right, I know you are. But, could we just hold off on putting it up, just for a little while?" She knew that with the lights on the deck, anyone down by the pond could easily tell where the deck ended. And even if they fell right in the water, it was shallow for a good two or three feet, so she really didn't see the need to ruin a great view by putting up the extra railing just yet.

Rory just nodded. "It's pretty much finished," he added. "Just let me know when you want it up and I'll take care of it." He wiped his hammer with a piece of cloth from his pocket and stowed it away carefully in a shiny blue toolbox. Annie recalled thinking that Rory's careful keeping of his tools had seemed a little odd, perhaps even OCD, when he'd first started working on the house. But she soon realized that Rory was careful with his tools like he was careful with the people around him. He was strongly of the opinion that if you take care of the things you care about, they'll take care of you, too.

Devon's voice broke her reverie. "Mom, Rory and I are going to run into town for some stuff from the hardware store. He says I can drive the truck--how cool is that?"

Annie forced a smile that she didn't feel onto her face. "That's totally cool," she lied. *Actually, the thought of my only child learning to drive makes me feel as uncool as humanly possible*, she thought, but kept her true feelings to herself. Devon deserved this. He needed some independence and she sure as heck didn't have the time or patience to teach him to drive. Rory's truck was old but reliable. And she was positive that Rory wouldn't let her son take any unnecessary chances on the road. He took care of his friends like he took care of his tools.

"I thought I'd go on and get a few things for our project," Rory winked at her. "You know, I kind of like the idea of building something from the ground up again. It's been a while since I built houses." Rory had been working with another carpenter for several years before Annie had returned to Coopersville. She wondered what kinds of houses he'd built in those years that she'd been away. She was sure that they must have been beautiful; he had a true gift when it came to carpentry and renovations.

"Would you mind picking up a few things for me, too? From the grocery store, I mean." Bessie had decided that the morning's drama called for pie and ice cream for dessert, and while Annie's mother always had the ingredients on hand for baking a pie, she didn't have the copious amounts of vanilla ice cream that would make it completely irresistible to the bed-and-breakfast's guests.

She explained what she needed and Rory made a quick list on his phone. "Where are they all now?" he asked, meaning her houseguests. "All over the place," she replied. "I'm not too worried about the Martins. They seem to be firmly planted in the sitting room," she laughed. "Kizzy and Rob can take care of themselves, I'm sure. I'm just not so sure about Mr. George and that Robichaud woman. She's a little flaky, to say the least, and he seems to be allergic to everything."

Devon scowled. "Yeah, he's allergic to TigerLily. Granny Bessie told me I have to keep her out of the sitting room while the guests are here," he added. Annie hadn't even thought about Devon's cat being an allergen for Mr. George. She would have to make sure she added a disclaimer to her website; the cat wasn't going anywhere. "And that phony psychic woman is a nutcase if you ask me."

"Devon, that's not nice," Annie chided.

"Yeah, I have to agree with Devon on this one." Rory shook his head. "She cornered me this morning and told me my aura was lonely. I think she's a few sandwiches short of a picnic."

"I heard her tell Kizzy that she is an internet psychic and she helps people contact their dead relatives. What a load of crap." Devon rolled his eyes. "Mom, you'd better be careful. You're turning into a real freak magnet."

Annie swiped at her son's arm playfully. "Well, I guess I'd better go check on my circus," she sighed. "Hopefully, no one else has died, found any dead bodies, or had their aura read by Marie."

She watched as Devon climbed behind the wheel of Rory's truck and prepared for his driving lesson, then she turned and headed back to the house, not wanting to watch her son grow up before her very eyes. She also feared that she'd left her mother unattended for too long, and hoped that the woman hadn't been stirring up some sort of mischief in Annie's absence.

8

Murder, Maybe

Annie's smartphone buzzed in her pocket as she reached the door leading into her kitchen from outside. Her heart moved itself up into her throat when she recognized Emmett's phone number on the screen. Surely he couldn't have the coroner's results so quickly.

"Hi, Emmett," Annie greeted him. "How's things?"

Emmett chuckled. "You sound like you're always expecting bad news, Annie. You should try expecting good news; it's a lot more fun."

Annie dared to relax, just a little. "So you're calling to tell me that my missing guest just took a tumble in the dark and there was no foul play involved?"

Emmett sighed. "Well, actually, no. He did take a tumble, but it looks like someone killed him before he hit the water. It wasn't a drowning," he explained. "No water in his lungs. I'm still waiting on the toxicology report, but the coroner says it looks like a case of anaphylactic shock."

"You mean like an allergic reaction?" Annie felt sick. She'd taken such care to make sure that the foods at the buffet had been kept separate for this very reason, despite the fact that her one allergic guest hadn't even been present. "Mr. Ross told me that he was allergic to nuts, so I made sure I kept those and the shellfish separate when I set out the food last night. And it was all gone when I went to bed," she added, "presumably before he ever arrived."

She thought about it for a moment, then began to relax. She had done everything right, she was certain of it. Perhaps Lou's death had simply been a tragic accident. "Sounds like you did everything you could to keep your guests safe," Emmett concluded. "However, I'm still not sure that Mr. Ross died of natural causes. At the very least, I don't think he died in that water."

Annie's mind tried to process what Emmett was hinting at. "You think someone dumped his body in the pond? Why?"

She could practically hear Emmett shaking his head through the phone. "Well, I just don't know. But I know a few people who would have liked to see Mr. Ross floating facedown in that pond. I ran his driver's license and prints through the database and, holy smokes, that man was wanted in a dozen different states. He had a list of prior offenses and suspected offenses as long as my arm," he added.

"What kind of offenses?" Annie couldn't believe what she was hearing. "You mean he was a criminal?" He had seemed so nice on the telephone. Annie shuddered to think that she'd almost let a wanted criminal stay in her home, then she felt extremely embarrassed for having had the thought. Rory had a criminal past. Granted, his was a one-time, drunken event, but who the heck was she to go judging people for having a criminal record?

"Well, now, seems like Mr. Ross was wanted for embezzlement, fraud, theft, and quite a few unpaid parking tickets." Emmett cleared his throat. "I'd say that Mr. Ross was a very active con artist, based on what I've read here."

"Wow." Annie leaned against the side of the house, swatting a fly from her face. It was hot, and she wanted to go inside, but she didn't want her guests to overhear her conversation with Emmett. She felt as though the Chief had just handed her a box filled with puzzle pieces, and she wanted to know exactly how they would fit together before she involved anyone else in the process. "So, for now, we're calling this a--a what? An accident, a murder, an accidental murder?"

"I'll let you know when I know," Emmett replied. "I just thought you ought to be aware of the circumstances surrounding the man's death, just in case you see anything else suspicious."

"You mean in case any of my other guests drop dead?" she replied with more than a hint of sarcasm.

"You're starting to sound like your mother, Annie Richards. Of course, I happen to like your mother, so I'm going to let that one slide," Emmett joked. "Just keep your eyes and ears open and let me know if you see any guests acting suspiciously. I'll call you as soon as I find out more information."

Annie and Emmett exchanged goodbyes. Her phone felt sweaty in her hand as she stepped into the cool air-conditioned kitchen. Bessie and Doris sat at the small kitchen table, snapping green beans. Annie was amazed at her mother's ability to get their paying guests actually to do work while enjoying their stay. She wondered whether she'd see Frank out in the yard mowing the grass next.

"Who was that on the phone, Annie?" Bessie asked as nonchalantly as possible, but Annie could tell she was chomping at the bit for information. "Have you heard anything from Emmett?"

Annie knew her mother so well. "Could I see you in the other room for just a minute, Mama?"

Bessie excused herself, leaving Doris cheerfully snapping beans and humming to herself.

"What are you doing asking our guests to prepare the food?" Annie tried sound annoyed, but she really didn't have the energy. Did she really even care if her guests wanted to help out?

"Oh, you grumpy thing," Bessie retorted, "she and I were just having the most fascinating chat. Did you know that the Martins are moving down here, possibly even to Coopersville?" Bessie's eyebrows were on high alert, trying to make Annie understand the importance of Bessie's bean-breaking conversation.

"And poor Doris told me that she and Frank had the worst thing happen to them last year. She told me that some scummy realtor took them for ten thousand dollars' worth of their savings. Isn't that awful?"

For a second, Annie forgot why she'd wanted to speak with her mother. "Wait--what? How does that even happen? You don't pay realtors any money."

"Oh, he wasn't even a real realtor," Bessie said in a hushed voice. "He was a conman! Doris told me that the police think he's done that to dozens of elderly people in their state. He told them that he could secure the house of their dreams and get them approved for a mortgage at less than one percent interest. Can you believe that?"

Annie shook her head in disbelief.

"Did you hear from Emmett?" Bessie asked again, moving on from her gossip to the topic she really wanted to talk about.

"Yes, as a matter of fact, I did." Annie pushed her chestnut hair behind her ears. "The man in the pond, the missing guest, he didn't drown." She waited for Bessie to react, but her mother said nothing. "Emmett isn't sure, but he thinks that the man died from an allergic reaction to something. He also thinks that his body was put in the pond after he died," she added and watched as Bessie's face became animated.

"I knew it!" she said, almost gleefully. "I mean, who drowns in two feet of water? Oh, Annie, you know what this means," she asked, putting one hand to her mouth for just a moment. "It means that we could have a killer in our midst." She nodded gravely.

Annie protested. "Hold on, Mama. Emmett told me that we shouldn't jump to any conclusions just yet. It'll be a little while before he gets all the information back from the coroner, so let's not do anything hasty. Besides, the last thing we want to do is scare the rest of our guests away with talk of murder. Let's just let the police do their job and keep a close eye on things here in the meantime."

Bessie agreed reluctantly. Annie knew that her mother probably wanted to discuss the matter at great length with her new friend, Doris, but Annie reminded her that if one of the guests did have something to do with Lou Ross's death, they still had no idea who it was. "I know you like Doris, but for now, the less she knows, the better. I suppose everyone's a suspect until we know more about how the man died."

Bessie returned to the kitchen and her bowl of beans while Annie went to her office. She sighed when she found a stack of papers had been knocked off her small desk. A cup holding pens and pencils had been knocked over on her desk and the empty cup bumped against her foot as she moved her chair. "Darned cat," Annie mumbled aloud, looking for any other evidence that TigerLily had been using her office as a playground.

She didn't see anything else out of place, so after sorting and straightening the papers and pens she pulled her clipboard out of her desk. It may have been an archaic way of keeping track of her guests, but Annie preferred keeping a printout of the business's guest list as well as any pertinent information about the guests that she wanted to remember. She didn't keep any financial information on the clipboard--that was all on her laptop--but she could tell at a glance when her guests would arrive and leave, whether they had any special dietary needs, and whether they'd be traveling alone.

Lou Ross's name jumped out at her. She'd had the page with his information on it at the top of the clipboard, anxiously awaiting her final guest's arrival. Now that she knew he wouldn't be staying with her, she was tempted to simply shred the document, though she knew she couldn't put the man out of her mind.

She moved his sheet to the back of the pile and reviewed her other guests' information. Kizzy was planning to stay until the end of the week, Rob had planned on leaving after only one night. She wondered why he'd changed his mind, but realized that he probably hoped that there'd be an opportunity for him to get a scoop on what happened to Mr. Ross.

Frank and Doris Martin were leaving a day after Kizzy. Annie thought that they had to be the best guests she could hope to ask for since they hadn't complained a single time and even seemed intent on helping out at the house. Her fingers slid across Alexander George's page, noting the numerous requests he'd made. Non-smoking room (they all were, luckily for him), hypoallergenic sheets, if possible, though he noted that he'd bring his own hypo-allergenic pillow, and he noted a preference for a room with few windows. Annie had thought this an odd request at the time, but since meeting the man, she realized that he was quite an odd fellow in general.

Marie Robichaud had simply inquired about WiFi connections and requested a room with a view. *Ah, Marie, doesn't every room have a view when you can see into the spirit world?* Annie chuckled aloud at the thought, then put the clipboard back in her desk drawer and retrieved a stack of bills from the same drawer, pulling the most current ones from the list and doing a quick mental calculation.

After a few minutes, Annie opened her laptop and began her least favorite task of the week. Paying bills had been bad enough when she ran a household of three, but now that her household was large enough to accommodate so many guests, the job was definitely more painful. She worked her way through the stack of paper bills, paying the ones that were absolutely due right that minute, then put the rest back into the drawer. She glanced at the clock on the computer screen and frowned. Time seemed to be in short supply these days, and Annie had just wasted forty minutes on paperwork and paying bills.

Annie swore to herself that she'd set up automatic payments on most of her bills once the business produced a steady income, but for now, the time-suck was a necessity, and so was keeping her guests happy, and alive. She rose from her chair and started to leave her office when she noticed a crumpled piece of paper lying just behind the door. *Darned cat must have been in the trash, too*, she thought.

Something bothered Annie as she reached for the paper. She almost always kept the office locked, and since the guests had arrived, she'd made extra sure that she did, for their safety as well as her privacy. After all, it wouldn't do to have guests nosing around in her paperwork, looking at information about other guests and possibly stumbling across financial information. Privacy laws were strict, even in a family-run inn, and Annie took her guests' privacy very seriously.

She checked for other signs that the cat had been in her

trash can, but only found the one scrap of paper. Curious, she unfolded the crumpled paper, expecting to find a receipt or scribbled budget sheet (she still preferred to do most of her budgeting by hand on paper--it just made everything seem more manageable). Instead, she found a handwritten note with Frank and Doris Martin's name and address written on it. Beneath this information someone had written a physical description of each of them, crude, but fairly accurate.

Annie stared at the strange note. She definitely hadn't written it, and she didn't recognize the handwriting. Instead of tossing the paper, she put it in her pocket and left the office, locking the door closed behind her.

As she turned to walk away, she nearly tripped over two of her guests. Rob and Kizzy were waiting for her outside of her office. She had no idea how long they'd been standing there.

"Annie, I'm sorry to bother you," Rob began, "but your mother said you were in the office. I just wanted to let you know that I spoke to Emmett." He lowered his voice. "It wasn't a drowning," he added, his voice just a notch above a whisper.

Annie nodded. "I know. I spoke with him earlier and he told me pretty much the same thing," she replied. "And I'm sure he told you the same thing he told me--not to panic and to just keep an eye out for strange or unusual things," she sighed.

"No offense, Mrs. Richards, but I've seen lots of strange and unusual things since I arrived," Kizzy interjected. "Like that Marie woman, and Mr. George. Those two are some strange birds," she giggled.

Annie smiled and suppressed a laugh. "Some of our guests are a little, erm, unusual, but I don't think that's what Emmett meant." She felt strange discussing the matter with Rob and slightly uncomfortable talking about it with Kizzy. She knew nothing about the woman, apart from the few things she'd gleaned from their short conversations. Kizzy seemed like an open book, but Annie reminded herself that she'd found the woman's phone at the same place she'd found Lou's body. Could she really be certain that Miss Fitzsimmons was as honest as she seemed?

"If you two will excuse me, I'm just going to go help my mother in the kitchen," Annie explained. "But I'll see you two at dinner. Bring your appetites," she added, "my mother is cooking a veritable feast."

Annie left her guests standing in the little space beside the stairs and took herself into the kitchen, where Bessie was now frying chicken alone. "Doris went upstairs to have a little nap," Bessie explained. "Poor thing's not used to all this country living," she added with a twinkle in her eye.

"Mama, you're not supposed to work our guests to death," Annie scolded, but she was secretly glad that Doris had been enlisted to prepare the beans. It wasn't Annie's favorite job, and at least she'd found the time to pay bills while the two older women tackled that particular kitchen duty.

"Oh, I don't think Doris minds one bit. And it's so good to have some friendly company my own age around here. No offense, but you can be a little bossy, darling." Bessie flipped the piece of chicken she was tending and grinned.

"Someone's got to keep you in line," Annie chuckled, happy to see her mother in such a happy, teasing mood. Annie realized that, despite the amount of work involved with running the inn, her family seemed to be thriving. Of course, it was early days yet, but Annie couldn't help but feel that her family had found its place in the world, and she actually looked forward to getting up every day to see what the day would bring.

Annie drained a pan of boiled potatoes and began mashing

them into submission. She heard the familiar crunch of tires on gravel as she blended them, and she glanced up only long enough to ascertain that it was Rory's truck pulling into its place out beside the barn. A few minutes later, as she spooned the mashed potatoes into a serving bowl, Annie discovered that her day wasn't through with surprises for her.

A yip and a yelp preceded her son through the back door. A dirty ball of fur with a tail like a motorboat propeller tried to escape her son's gangly teenage arms. The smell of dog suddenly overpowered the scent of fried chicken. Devon grinned from ear to ear, carrying a new houseguest.

9

Angry Guests and Pie

"Can we keep him?" Devon struggled to keep the wriggling pup from breaking free. It squirmed and whined, sniffing the air furiously and seeking out the source of the fried chicken's aroma.

"What on earth--" Annie began, "Where did you find that?"

"Well, it wasn't on our list," Rory said, following Devon with an armful of shopping bags, "but the little guy was just sitting by the side of the road looking so forlorn. We had to stop and grab him. Somebody would have probably hit him with their car if we hadn't." He handed the bags to Annie, who had wiped her hands on a towel and was now examining the dog for a collar.

"No collar," Devon confirmed, "so we can keep him, right?"

"Not so fast," Annie countered, "He might be microchipped. We should take him to the vet's office and check," she suggested.

"Oh, Dr. Fisher isn't open this late," Bessie said, sneaking the dog a piece of fried chicken she'd pinched off of the bone. "Besides, this little guy looks like he's been mistreated. I mean, look, he's skin and bones!" She continued to fuss over the pup until Annie put her foot down.

"He has to get out of this kitchen." She looked at Devon, who was still silently pleading with eyes as large as the pup's own big brown ones. "Go put him up out in the barn for now. Give him some cat food and water and we'll take him to Dr. Fisher first thing in the morning."

"And if he doesn't have a chip?" Devon asked anxiously.

"Then Dr. Fisher can find him a good home," Annie replied, feeling only a little bit like a traitor.

"We can give him a home," Devon countered, not willing to let the subject go.

Annie started to say something, but Rory cut her off. "Now, Devon, let's just go do as your mom asked. I'm sure this little guy is hungry."

Devon's shoulders slumped slightly as he turned to follow Rory out the door. Annie was sure that she heard Rory say something about changing her mind as they walked away.

"What about that?" Bessie said, shaking her head. "Poor little guy, just left on the side of the road like that. I don't see how people can be so cruel."

Annie couldn't understand it, either. From the look of the puppy, it couldn't have been more than a three or four months old. "I guess we're starting to get a reputation for taking in orphans," She replied, half-jokingly.

"So you're going to let him keep the dog?" Bessie asked, but it sounded more like a statement.

"Do you really think I have a choice?" Annie replied with a grin. "As long as he doesn't belong to anyone else, I don't have a problem with it. Besides, it might be nice to have a guard dog around here. If we'd had one the other night, Mr. Ross might not have ended up in the pond the way he did."

The two women washed up and began carrying plates filled with food to the dining room. Annie had already set the long dining table with plates, cutlery, and glasses. They piled the table high with dishes full of fried chicken, freshly baked biscuits, green beans, mashed potatoes, corn on the cob, coleslaw and freshly sliced tomatoes and cucumbers, which were Bessie's favorite. Their guests could simply help themselves to the food, like one big family sitting down for the evening meal.

They'd told everyone that dinner would be ready by six, and although it was only a quarter to, the scent of food drew her guests into the dining room like music from the Pied Piper's merry pipe. Annie was starving, so she knew her guests must be hungry, too.

The guests piled their plates high with the food, praising Bessie's culinary skills through full mouths. "Where's your boy?" Frank Martin asked around a bite of fried chicken. "He's a bright kid," he added before washing it down with tea.

"Oh, he and Rory are eating out on the veranda. It seems that they picked up a new guest when they ran some errands for me," she replied. "They found a puppy," she explained. "I told them to keep it outside for now, but I'm sure it will find its way into my son's bedroom before the day is over."

"Aww," Kizzy gushed, "how sweet! Did they just find it outside?"

"It was on the side of the road," Annie clarified. "People drop strays off all the time out here in the countryside. It's sad, really. Most of them get hit by cars or end up starving to death." Annie had made sure that they'd visited the vet as soon as they were settled in the house to have Devon's cat, TigerLily, spayed. She definitely didn't want to add to the unwanted pet population, and the young cat was enough trouble on her own. Annie couldn't imagine how much trouble adding a puppy to her household was going to be.

"Dogs are a lot of work," Mr. George interjected, and Annie was surprised to hear him trying to join the conversation. "I had a dog when I was a boy, but he died."

"Oh, I'm sorry to hear that," Annie replied, not quite sure of how to respond.

"Don't be. Dogs die, you know. People die, too." Alexander George chewed his biscuit thoughtfully. "It's all part of the circle of life. These biscuits are wonderful, Mrs. Purdy."

An uncomfortable lull in the conversation threatened to settle in, but Rob stepped up and broke the silence. "I can't help but feel we're all in some weird little play," he suggested. "You know, like one of those Agatha Christie dinner theater productions."

Kizzy giggled. "Oh, I've always wanted to do one of those. I did a play at the local dinner theater in my hometown," she added. "But it was a comedy." She sighed. "I just had a bit part, but it was fun."

"I know exactly how he feels," Marie added. "I'm sure that Robert is feeling the same thing that I do," she continued. Rob cringed at her use of his full name.

"And what is that?" he asked, baffled.

"The spirits, of course. Oh, they are restless here! I sensed something very old when I first arrived, but after that gentleman died in the pond, well, the spirits are very disturbed, indeed."

Annie pursed her lips. "I'm not sure I believe in spirits. I haven't seen any ghosts around here if that's what you mean."

Marie clucked her tongue. "Oh, no, ghosts are entirely different. They're usually just noisy, a nuisance, really. I'm talking about angry souls who died before their time. Don't you feel it? That tension in the air when you enter an empty room, or that feeling that someone is watching you when you are alone--that is a spirit trying to make its presence known. I think that Lou Ross is trying to tell us something about who murdered him, and we should definitely listen."

"Well, the police aren't so sure that he was murdered, Miss Robichaud," Annie replied, putting her fork down on her plate.

Rob cleared his throat. "Actually, that's precisely why it feels like we're in an Agatha Christie story. Emmett said the death *could have* been accidental, but there's no proof of that, either. A mysterious death, a room full of strangers--I'm waiting for Angela Lansbury to pop up any minute now and tell us all whodunnit."

"Do you think a ghost killed Mr. Ross?" Kizzy suggested, suppressing a giggle. "Maybe Marie here can contact him *beyond the grave* and just tell the police what happened."

"You laugh, but vengeful spirits are not to be teased. I've been working with the spirit world for many years, and I've seen what happens when people don't take them seriously," Marie warned, her eyes flaring. "I've seen strong men grow sick and weak, sane people turn crazed from fear, all because they didn't believe that spirits could harm them. Perhaps I should perform a cleansing ritual for your home, Annie?"

"Thank you, but I don't think that will be necessary," Annie replied.

"Do the police know any more about the dead man, Annie? Who he was, or if he has any next of kin?" Doris had a gentle look of concern on her face, and Annie could tell she was trying to steer the conversation into saner waters.

"According to the Chief of Police, the man was a wanted criminal," Rob replied before Annie could say anything. She flashed him a look that she hoped would make him see sense and shut his mouth, but he kept talking. Obviously, Rob's idea of not making hasty conclusions included solving the crime all on his own.

"Emmett said that he was a conman, Mrs. Martin. I've been

looking into the guy's past, and he wasn't a very nice man, by the look of things." Rob leaned back in his chair, confidently posing as though he was giving his own newscast. "Sources say that Lou Ross ran savings and lending scams that targeted elderly and disabled people. Pretty scummy, if you ask me."

"Well, then maybe he deserved to die," Frank said coldly. "People like that, they get what they deserved if you ask me." He gritted his teeth and took a long swig of his ice water.

"Frank!" Doris' cheeks flushed and her eyes narrowed. "What a horrible thing to say! Of course, you don't mean that. We're not that kind of people," she added, apologizing to the room for her husband's statement.

"Speak for yourself, Doris. If I could get my hand on that piece of scum...I'd kill him with my own two hands."

The room fell silent once again. Frank rose from the table. "I'm sorry if I've upset anyone, Mrs. Richards. I'm going to go step outside and get some fresh air. These kinds of things--well, they get to me," he said, struggling to explain himself.

"It's alright, Mr. Martin. Please help yourself to one of my rocking chairs on the front porch. They're perfect for de-stressing," Annie replied lamely.

After Frank had left the table, Bessie tried to change the conversation. "I hope you all saved some room for dessert," she scolded playfully. "We've got homemade blackberry pie, peach cobbler, and ice cream." She grinned at the guests, "I know you'll love it!"

Doris couldn't let things lie. "I'm so sorry about Frank--he's just still so angry about last year."

"What happened last year?" Kizzy asked, reaching for a tooth-pick.

"Oh, it was awful," Doris began, shaking her head. "There was

73

a man, John Dawes, or so he called himself. We had been looking online for retirement properties and he claimed to be able to help us find the home of our dreams. He told us that he'd do all the traveling, he'd take photos, talk to the sellers, and handle everything for us so we could just stay home and wait for the perfect place.

"Well, he was so nice, and he promised us such a good interest rate on our mortgage--said he had an arrangement with the bank--so we didn't think twice when he told us that he needed ten thousand dollars in cash. He said it was to cover a down payment, plus some of his travel expenses. We thought it was more than fair, but then things went wrong. After we wired him the money, his emails and phone calls became less frequent. Then they stopped." She clenched her jaw. "That man took ten thousand dollars of our hard-earned savings and just vanished."

"Oh," Kizzy breathed, "that's awful! I guess I'd have to agree with your husband," she added, "maybe some people deserve to end up face down in a pond."

Doris smiled, but it was empty. "Yes, Kizzy, I'm sure that wherever Mr. Dawes is, karma will take care of him. At least, that's what I keep telling myself. And now, here we are, looking at moving down here to South Carolina. It all works out in the end," she said, trailing off.

"Please, excuse me, too," Mr. George said abruptly. "I need to go to my room for a bit. I'm afraid my allergies are acting up and I must put my drops in my eyes." He didn't wait for anyone to reply, he simply rose and left the table.

"He is so weird!" Kizzy whispered loudly as Alexander disappeared from sight. "Does anybody know what he does for a living?"

"He told me he works at the post office," Rob replied.

"Well, if he goes postal, I wouldn't want to be around," Kizzy laughed.

"Why don't I bring out the pie and ice cream?" Bessie suggested, trying to steer the conversation back to something more comfortable.

"I'll help you, Mama," Annie added, scooting her chair away from the table. "You all sit, enjoy yourselves. We'll have the dessert out in no time," she added over her shoulder as she was walking away. Annie let out a deep breath as she left the room. Her mother could manage the dessert on her own just fine, but Annie needed an excuse to get away from everyone for just a few minutes. Dinner had been almost as stressful as finding Lou Ross' body, and she still had dessert to get through. She could hear her mother scolding Devon's cat in the kitchen.

Annie decided to step out onto the front porch for just a moment before heading back into the dining room. Maybe she'd do what she'd advised Frank to do and enjoy a few minutes in one of the rocking chairs. She stepped out into the cool evening air and was greeted by the sound of crickets. A gentle breeze cooled her cheeks as she scanned the porch for her guest. He wasn't out here.

She could hear Devon's laughter carrying on the wind, so she decided to check the back veranda. Probably Frank had joined him and Rory out back. She cut through the house, stopping just long enough to make sure her mother didn't actually need her and made her way to the back porch. It was empty, too, but there was someone on the deck by the pond.

Annie peered through the darkened screen at the figure by the pond. It was Frank Martin, and he appeared to be looking for something in the water.

10

Suspicions, Spirits, and Skeptics

Annie watched Frank for a few minutes, taking care to not be seen. She didn't want him to think that she was spying on him, but she supposed that she actually *was* spying on him. After a few minutes, he gave up on looking for whatever it was he'd been searching for and headed up the hill towards the barn.

From the light coming out of the barn's open door, Annie guessed that Rory and Devon were inside, probably tending to the puppy they'd found. She made a mental note to talk to Rory later about Frank, then headed back into the house.

She had gotten no further than the kitchen when her phone rang, making her jump a little. Annie pulled out the phone, barely registering the fact that it was Emmett's number calling her once again. "Hello?"

"Annie, Emmett here. Gotta quick question for you: do you know if Lou Ross had a dog?"

Annie thought for a minute. "I don't know," she replied hesitantly. "If he did, he didn't mention it to me. Why would he?"

"Well, forensics found dog hair all over the front seat of Mr. Ross's car and there was a near-empty bag of dog food shoved up under one of the seats. The funny thing is, when we went through the items in the car, it didn't look like Lou was going on vacation."

"It didn't?"

"Nope. It looked like he was leaving town. The guy had what looked like everything he owned in that car, what little that was. And he was travelling with quite a bit of interesting paperwork," Emmett added with a whistle. "Fake passports, driver's licenses, you name it--he sure was a busy fella."

Annie shook her head. "Did you happen to find anything about the people he conned?" She thought about what Doris had told everyone at dinner. "I think I should tell you that two of my guests were victims of a con man last year," she added, hoping that Emmett would tell her that it wasn't likely that her guests were ever involved with the despicable Mr. Ross.

"You mean the Martins?" Emmett had been busy, indeed. "I didn't want to say anything just yet, I was hoping you'd have some time to watch your guests for a little bit and see if you spotted any unusual behavior, but since you seem to know something, I'll fill you in on what we know.

"Ross kept cryptic notes on his victims, as far as we can tell. There was a laptop in the car, but we haven't been able to get into that yet. Once we've gotten in there and retrieved all the information from that we'll have a better idea of what we're dealing with, but we did find notes that could have been about the Martins.Then again, he may have never had a thing to do with their situation. Like I said, it'll take a while to put things together, but I'd venture a guess and say that if the Martins knew that a scam artist was staying there, they wouldn't be too happy."

Annie thought about Frank's angry outburst at dinner and his unusual behavior afterwards. It wasn't enough to prove that he'd known Lou was at Rosewood Place, but it still made her feel uncomfortable. "Have the Martins seen the body?"

"No," Emmett replied, "but I may drop by your place sometime to talk to a couple of your guests. I'd like to speak to Miss Fitzsimmons again and maybe show the Martins a picture of Lou Ross."

Annie thought of the phone she'd found on the deck. "Why do you want to speak to Kizzy?"

"Well, the victim's prints were found on her phone and she was the last person at the scene of the crime. It might be circumstantial, but I'd like to talk to her again, rule some things out," he replied casually. Annie knew that Emmett never took anything lightly, so if he wanted to interview her guests again, he must have strong suspicions about who really killed Mr. Ross.

"Well, I won't keep you," he added, and Annie could hear him shuffling in his seat. "I just wanted to ask about the dog while it was on my mind. Of course, it could be absolutely unimportant, but you know what they say--sometimes the things that seem unimportant are actually crucial to solving a crime."

Annie had no idea who 'they' were, but Emmett's logic sounded solid. "Wait, Emmett. I do know something about a dog. Might not be the same one, but like you said, little things, right?"

She told him about the puppy that Rory and Devon found. "Did you take him up to see Dr. Fisher yet?" he asked. "Might have one of those microchips in it."

"Not yet, but we're going first thing in the morning," she replied. "We can swing by the police station if you want to see the dog."

"Alright, I guess we could take a fur sample," he chuckled, "maybe run the dog's pawprints to see if he's been in any trouble with the law."

Annie groaned. "I'll call you if I see anything unusual," she replied, ignoring his joke.

"Oh, and there's one more thing," Emmett added. "We're not yet sure if Ross was alone when he arrived at your place. It looks like he was working with someone, but he uses codenames in his notes. Once we get into that laptop we might be able to get more information. We're working on getting his cell phone records, too. He could have been working with someone right up until he was killed, and if so, that person is definitely a suspect, and likely to be a dangerous one."

Annie frowned. "If he brought someone with him, where did they go? It's not a short walk to get anywhere from my place," she asked.

"Might not have brought them," he replied. "His accomplice could have already been there, waiting for him." His statement made Annie's spine tingle with cold. It was bad enough that one of her guests could have murdered Lou, but the possibility that one of them waited patiently for him to arrive, mingled amiably with Annie and her other guests, and then killed the man in cold blood, was more than she could stomach.

"Emmett, you come on by anytime you want to talk to my guests. I'll let you know if I see anything out of the ordinary."

"Thanks, Annie. And I guess it goes without saying, but be careful. If there's a murderer staying at your bed-and-breakfast, they're hanging around for a reason. If we can figure out what that reason is, we might be able to catch them before anyone else gets hurt."

Annie felt a chill despite the August heat as she ended the call with Emmett. She considered each of her guests, trying to decide if any one of them seemed more suspicious to her than the others. Frank's unusual behavior at dinner gnawed at her, but before that he'd seemed so friendly and relaxed. And Emmett seemed to think that Kizzy could still be a suspect. Did the bubbly blonde even have it in her to kill someone?

Annie's head spun with questions. She didn't want to think that a killer was sleeping peacefully under her roof. She sighed. She'd always wanted to run a bed-and-breakfast. Her dream of taking care of others in her own home had finally come true. She just never dreamed that taking care of them would mean keeping them safe from cold-blooded killers, especially when the killer was likely to be one of them.

Annie's heart nearly leapt from her chest when a bony finger tapped her on her left shoulder. She spun around to find Marie peering at her intently. Annie had no idea how long the woman had been standing there, but it made her feel extremely uncomfortable to think that she may have overheard Annie's conversation with Emmett.

"Mrs. Richards," Marie began, twisting a strand of beads that circled her neck. "I just wanted to tell you again how lovely I think your home is. As an inn, well, it's quite cozy, but I can't help but wish you'd heed my earlier warnings about the spirits here. I have seen things," she confessed, peering into Annie's eyes cryptically, "that would make your hair stand on end. I understand if you don't believe me yet," she sniffed, "but just don't say you weren't warned."

Marie's words hung in the air between them for a long moment. Annie didn't want to offend the woman--she clearly believed every word of her own speech--but Annie had never been superstitious and had no plans to get spooked now.

"I appreciate your concern, Miss Robichaud, but really, I don't think there's anything I can do about spirits right now. At the moment, our main concern should be helping the police figure out what happened to Mr. Ross. I don't even know if he had any relatives who might be missing him, and that worries me just a little more than the possibility of his restless spirit hanging around."

Marie nodded slowly. "Mr. Reynolds says that the man was a criminal. Perhaps he left no one who mourns him," she suggested. "All the same, it's not uncommon for those who die suddenly to have some sort of unfinished business, something that they need to see taken care of, even after they are dead."

"Well, I guess we'll just never know," Annie replied, shaking her head. "It's not like he left behind a lot of information about himself." She tried to understand why Marie was so fixated with the idea of Lou's spirit hanging around. "What is it that you do again, Miss Robichaud? You're a medium, right?"

Marie smiled. "Yes, that's right. I have a deep connection to the spirit world and I can often sense things that others can't. It's a gift and a curse, I can assure you. But I can tell you that not all spirits go easily into the afterlife. I've seen very bad things happen when spirits are angry about their deaths, and I just thought I should warn you so you'd know what to look out for."

Annie was sceptical, but she didn't want to offend Marie. Perhaps the woman was telling the truth, or at least her version of it, but Annie didn't want to start looking for answers in the supernatural realm. "And what is it that I should know?"

"I've seen angry spirits burn entire buildings to the ground," Marie replied, "I've seen people become suddenly, inexplicably ill in the presence of a vengeful spirit, and I've seen what some would call accidents, but what I would call the act of a soul who is not yet ready to be departed from this world," she finished gravely. "Don't discount the possibilities, Annie. Never underestimate the power of the supernatural." Annie must have looked unconvinced, because Marie continued. "Do you believe in life after death? That those who have died can communicate with the living?"

Annie thought about this for a long moment. It would be nice to believe that death wasn't the end of things, and it was a pleasant thought that her father's spirit might be watching over her even in the form of a solemn little redbird. She thought about the diary of Rose Cooper, how it and a letter from Rose's brother had spoken to her hundreds of years after their deaths. It wasn't quite the same thing, but it was the type of afterlife communication that Annie felt most comfortable believing.

"I'm not sure what I think," she replied finally. "But I am certain that we shouldn't be worrying everyone or causing hysterics by suggesting that there's an evil spirit running amok on this plantation." Annie sighed. "Miss Robichaud, I do appreciate your concern, but for now, I'm going to focus on assisting the police with their investigation. Have you had dessert yet? My mother's blackberry pie is practically blue ribbon," she finished, changing the subject.

Marie opened her mouth to say something, but she closed it again, silenced for the moment by the approach of Frank. "Mrs. Richards! Mrs. Richards, could I speak to you for a minute?"

Annie turned to see Frank marching across her lawn towards the veranda. He was slightly out of breath from the walk, and she could see that he was sweating profusely. He definitely wasn't used to *country living*, as her mother would say.

Annie left Marie on the veranda and met the man halfway. "Oh, boy! I don't think I've walked this much in years," he confessed, catching his breath. "Just went up to the barn," he explained, "talked to Rory and your boy. That's a good looking little dog they found," he added, nodding his head for emphasis. "I asked Rory about the fishing in these parts," he continued. "He said I might be able to get a fishing pole and a temporary fishing license in town, is that right?"

Annie nodded. "Actually, I probably have a pole you can borrow out in the shed. And you don't need a fishing license to fish in my pond since it's on private property."

"You mean there are fish in the pond?" Frank looked a little sceptical. "I didn't see any when I looked down by the deck there."

"Oh, yes, there are a ton of fish in there. It's a fully stocked pond and I've caught many fish myself in there," she added. "But you really don't want to fish by the deck. All the big fish are around on the other side of the pond. You have to go around and through the woods to get to my favorite spot. Or, you could take our little boat. It's just a two-seater, but it's perfect for rowing out and drowning a few worms," she added, happy for an explanation about what the man had been doing down on the deck earlier.

"Do you think I could borrow that fishing rod tomorrow? I'd love to do a bit of fishing, and I'm afraid that Doris is going to have me looking at houses soon if I don't find some ways to keep out of her hair," he laughed.

Annie felt in her pocket for her keys. "Here, let me go check the shed and make sure those fishing rods are in there. If they are, I can have Rory show you the spot where we like to fish and you can head up there first thing in the morning, before it gets too hot."

She led the man over to the small, prefabricated shed behind the barn. She unlocked the door, stowing the lock in her back pocket while she dug through gardening tools and an assortment of outdoor clutter that had accumulated over the summer. A bag of charcoal and a container of lighter fluid sat in one corner of the shed, reminding her that she really ought to fire up the grill at least once while her guests were at the house. Summer wouldn't last forever, so she might as well make the most of her grill.

"Ah, here they are," she said, at last, pulling a bucket of fishing rods out of a far corner. Frank's eyes lit up at the bundle of rods and reels.

"You must really love your fishing," he commented. "There must be a dozen fishing rods in there."

Annie laughed. "No, only about nine or ten. Some of these were my father's," she explained. "And a couple are my mom's and Devon's. This one," she said, pulling a teal-colored rod from the bunch, "is mine. I don't use it often enough," she lamented, "which is a shame because, well, I have all this in my backyard." She selected a rod for Frank and handed it to him. It was burgundy and silver, well-worn and much-used. "That one was one of Dad's. He would have loved this place," she said, a sad smile on her lips.

"Your mother has mentioned him a few times," Frank said. "He sounds like a great guy."

"Oh, he was," Annie assured him. "He was the best. He died a little over five years ago, but I swear, sometimes I feel like he's still right here with me." She pulled the bucket to the front of the shed and returned the two rods. "I'll just leave these right here so we can get to them easily in the morning. That way, you can just grab one and go," she smiled.

Annie noticed that Marie was watching them as she re-locked the shed. Frank noticed, too. "What do you make of that loon?" he asked, not bothering to hide his opinion of Marie. "I can't stand all that ghosts and ghouls mumbo-jumbo. If you ask me, those so-called mediums are just as bad as the con artists that steal people's money."

Annie considered this for a minute. "I suppose some people are just looking for a little hope," she replied finally. "They're hoping for proof that there's something after this life. I can see how it could be comforting for someone to tell you that your lost loved ones are safe and happy, waiting for you to come to them."

Frank rolled his eyes. "Yeah, and those so-called psychics are full of hope that you'll be foolish enough to hand over your wallet to them so your money can cross over to the other side, too," he snorted. "Don't get me wrong, I'm willing to believe in ghosts and an afterlife. I just don't believe anyone who tells me they've got a direct line to the other side."

Marie waved to Annie, a vacant smile on her face. Annie waved back. "Let's go inside and see if there's any pie left. I'd hate for you to miss out on my mother's dessert," she said, ending the conversation. She started back up towards the house and Frank followed behind, much less agitated than he'd been when he'd stormed out of the dining room. Annie breathed a sigh of relief and hoped that she'd seen the last of the drama for the day, but something in her gut told her she needed to be ready for more, just in case.

11

Barking Up Trees

"You're going to have to let that dog sleep in the house," Rory advised Annie, "or nobody's getting any sleep."

She covered her ears, drowning out the high-pitched whine coming from the barn. "I doubt they can hear it in the house," she replied. "Besides, he could always sleep with you in your camper," she teased.

Rory grinned. "Oh, no, Annie Purdy, you are not pushing that trouble onto me."

"Wait a minute, Rory Jenkins," she countered, ignoring his familiar use of her maiden name. "You're the one who brought the dog home. If anybody's going to play mother dog, it should be you."

"Actually, it was Devon's idea, but since you're such a mean mom and you won't let the little fella out there sleep in the house, I guess you're responsible for the crying." He crossed his arms and waited for her reply.

Annie laughed. "You can't antagonize me, Rory. Mean mom, my foot. I let you two keep it in the barn, didn't I?"

Rory grinned. "You know I have to give you a hard time. Otherwise, I risk losing my cool dude status with the young people around here," he laughed, leaning back in his chair and stretching out his long, muscular legs. Annie caught herself admiring his tanned legs and comparing them to her own milky white ones, which were definitely not muscular. She made a silent promise to herself that she'd start walking every day once the weather cooled down. The last thing the lodging house needed was an owner who was too out of shape to keep up with the guests, she reckoned.

They sat in a companionable silence for a minute, the sound of crickets and a howling dog filling the night air around them. "I talked to Mr. Martin for a little bit today," he said at last. "Seems like a nice fella. Tightly wound, though."

Annie nodded. "I think he's been under a lot of stress for a while. He and his wife had a hard time last year." She explained what Doris had told her about the con man stealing their money.

"That's pretty awful," he replied. "I hate to hear that. It just goes to show you that there are way too many scumbags out there willing to steal money from decent people."

Annie realized that she hadn't had a chance to tell Rory about her conversation with Emmett. "I nearly forgot--Emmett called me. That guy, the one who died? He was a con artist. Emmett says he was wanted in several states and had a rap sheet a mile long."

Rory sat up straight. "What?"

"Emmett says that he may have even been meeting someone here." She stopped short at adding the part about a possible murder, but Rory was quick enough to put two and two together.

"Do you think he was killed in some sort of double-cross, or maybe it was a revenge situation? I mean, you just told me that the Martins got conned out of ten thousand dollars. Maybe Frank decided to get some revenge."

"Ssshhh," Annie hissed. "I don't want one of the guests coming out here and hearing this. Emmett thinks that Lou Ross died from anaphylactic shock. When he called to book his room, he did mention that he had a nut allergy, so that makes sense."

Rory thought for a moment. "If that guy was working with someone, who was it?" He waited for Annie to make a suggestion, but she just shrugged. "Annie, if it was one of your guests--"

"If if was one of my guests, then I have to be extra careful what I say around them," she replied, cutting him off. "And I have to hope that Emmett and the rest of the police department are quick in finding out who it is." She reached out and put a hand on his arm. "And he will find out," she reassured him, "but he has to be discreet. If the killer thinks someone's on to him or her, they could run. Or panic," she added.

"Would that be a bad thing?" he asked. "I mean, it would be better for you if the killer just up and left, right?"

Annie hesitated. "It might be better for our safety, but there would still be a killer at large, only then Emmett wouldn't have any idea of how to find them."

"But they killed a bad guy," Rory countered, "someone who conned people out of their money for a living."

"It doesn't matter who they killed," she replied, her voice firm. "Murder is murder. What I'd love to know is why they killed him," she added.

"If we knew that, we'd probably know who the killer was," Rory pointed out. "If Frank killed him, which I doubt, one could argue that it's justifiable homicide," he joked. "If Lou's partner in crime killed him, it was probably over money or a woman."

Annie looked at him quizzically. "Why do you say that?"

"Most crimes of passion are about romances that have gone wrong," Rory replied. "People do crazy things when their hearts get broken."

Annie thought about this for a minute. She'd moved across the country and started a new life when her heart had been broken. She hadn't killed her dead husband's mistress, though she'd certainly thought about it. "Well, if it was a passion crime, who's to say it was a woman that did the deed? We don't know if Lou Ross was into women or men," she added.

"True. So everyone's a suspect," Rory agreed. "That is totally *not* helpful."

They sat there in silence for a few minutes, each contemplating the death of Lou Ross. Eventually, Annie realized that it had become exceedingly quiet. "I think he's settling down now," she ventured, gesturing towards the barn and the previously howling dog.

She was about to remark on how glad she was that the dog had stopped crying when she heard barking from inside the house. "What the--"

Annie and Rory both rose from their rocking chairs at the same time and headed for the sound. She hadn't even got the door opened all the way when she saw the little dog--in Devon's arms-- barking furiously at something just out of sight. She stepped further into the house and followed the dog's line of sight but saw nothing.

"What on earth are you doing?" She stared at her son, waiting impatiently for an answer. The dog continued to bark, struggling against Devon's grip. It seemed to Annie that the pup wanted desperately to get into the sitting room, so she peered around the doorway and into the room. Marie was inside, sitting in a chair and reading a book. She smiled up at Annie.

"Everything all right, Annie? That little dog seems awfully upset."

"Everything is fine, Marie. Sorry to bother you, my son was just putting the puppy to bed."

Annie returned her attention to the dog. It was no longer filthy, at least. Devon must have washed the pup at some point. *That might explain the whining earlier*, she thought. She approached the pup and tried to help calm it, but it seemed determined to get into the sitting room. It struggled and strained, barking and growling. If the puppy had been bigger, he might have succeeded at breaking loose, but since he was small, the effect was comical. Loud, but still quite funny.

"Mom, I gave him a bath. I just--he was crying. I couldn't leave him outside all alone." Devon made his eyes big, rivaling the pup's for sincerity. "Just for tonight."

"His barking is going to keep the guests awake," Annie replied, ignoring her son's pleading.

"He wasn't barking in the kitchen," Devon countered, "he only started when I got to the stairs. He must have heard something weird in there," he added, nodding towards the sitting room and giving his mother a knowing glance.

"It's getting late. People will be going to sleep soon, and I don't want to have to apologize for a barking dog all night."

"Mom, listen. Let me take him to my room. If he keeps barking, I'll put him in the barn again and take my sleeping bag out there so he won't be lonely. I promise that if he doesn't stop barking in like, ten minutes, I'll take him back outside."

Annie sighed. "Five minutes and you are not sleeping out in that barn." She gave the growling puppy a scratch behind his ear and watched her son ascend the stairs. As soon as they were out of sight the dog stopped barking.

Rory let out a low whistle. "That dog was not happy about something," he said, stating the obvious. "I wonder what could have set him off?"

Annie had an uncomfortable feeling in her stomach. Probably it was the stress of a barking dog after dealing with the day's events, but she couldn't help shake the feeling that she was missing something important about the dog's outburst. "I guess I should just be glad that he's stopped barking," she replied. "At least the cat doesn't make that kind of noise."

"That's because your cat would gladly hand you all over to an axe murderer if she got cat treats out of the trade," Rory replied. "Dogs are loyal and protective, and it looks like that one has taken a shine to Devon."

Annie didn't want to agree with Rory, but the pup had seemed to be trying to protect Devon from some unseen threat. She hated to admit it, but TigerLily would have run and hid in a heartbeat. "Well, let's hope Dr. Fisher gives us good news about the pup in the morning, eh?" She rubbed her temples, feeling the beginning pangs of a headache coming on.

"I'm going to leave you under the protection of that ferocious beast," Rory joked, "and bid you goodnight. I'll see you in the morning, Miss Purdy."

Annie yawned, surprised by how tired she suddenly felt. She watched him step back out through the front door. "See you in the morning, Mr. Jenkins." She pushed the door closed behind him, then turned and headed up the stairs to her own bedroom for what she hoped would be a peaceful night's sleep.

12

Where There's Smoke

Annie sighed in her sleep. She dreamed she was back in New York, just visiting, and shopping on Fifth Avenue. In her dream, she had a wallet that was so full of cash that she couldn't close it. Her mother was in the dream, too, picking out lovely, lovely things to take back to Rosewood Place. Annie ran her hand across a pair of silk curtains and admired their delicate beauty.

"Aren't these gorgeous?" the dreaming woman asked her mother. The gentle sound of elevator music filled the room and Dream Annie could just make out a hint of fragrance drifting on the air, probably from the perfume counter.

"I smell smoke." Dream Bessie's words were cheerfully inconsistent with the rest of Annie's dream.

Dream Annie stared at Dream Bessie. "What?" She looked around the Saks department store, but she didn't see any smoke. She did see some darling pillows and a dreamy floral comforter set.

"Something's burning, dear. Wake up." Bessie smiled in the dream, but her words didn't sound happy. Dream Annie frowned as her subconscious started piecing together her mother's words. She didn't want to wake up, but soon, her eyes fluttered open.

Real Bessie was standing beside Annie's bed, her eyes filled with barely contained panic and her hands holding a glass of water. "Annie, the deck is on fire!"

Annie was out of bed before she'd even sat up properly. Her bedroom window overlooked the backyard and most of the pond, including the deck. She pulled back her curtain, hoping her mother had just dreamed about a fire. An orange glow greeted her and she just had time to glimpse the outline of a person rushing towards the burning deck. Rory.

He had a bucket in his hand and was scooping water from the pond onto the fire, which thankfully seemed to only be on one end of the deck.

"We need to go help him," Bessie whispered, reminding Annie that there were guests sleeping in the next room. Bessie lifted her glass to reiterate her point.

"Let's go," Annie agreed, taking her mother's glass and sitting it on the bedside table. "You're going to need a bigger glass," she said, pulling on her slippers and moving past the elder woman.

"This isn't for the fire," Bessie replied, annoyance creeping into her voice. "I was going to throw it on you. I almost couldn't wake you. You sleep like the dead, you know."

They snuck downstairs and out the back door, trying to be as quiet as possible. Annie remained calm, which wasn't easy. Fire was bad news for her business. If murder wasn't enough to keep guests away, inexplicable fires would surely do the trick.

"How did you know that there was a fire?" she asked Bessie, stopping in the kitchen to grab the bucket they used for mopping the floors.

"I just happened to glance out my window when I got up to go to the bathroom," Bessie explained. "It was just pure luck," she added, shaking her head.

By the time they reached Rory, he had the fire almost completely out. "What happened?" Annie's bucket hung limply at her side. "Are you okay?"

Rory wiped soot from his hand onto his shirt, then he rubbed his eyes and nose, which still stung from the smoke. "Somebody set the deck on fire." His tone was certain.

"What?" Bessie's mouth fell open. "How do you know?"

Rory pointed at the spot where the fire had been. The entire end of the deck was black and charred, burned through in a few places. "The fire was just in that one spot, right by the water. And can you smell that?" He sniffed the air, squinting his eyes in concentration.

Annie answered. "Lighter fluid." Her mind raced back to earlier in the evening, the storage shed and Frank asking about the fishing rods. Wordlessly, she headed for the shed, stumbling in the inky darkness.

"Annie?" her mother called after her, and Rory followed.

The door to the shed was closed, but the lock was off, lying useless on the ground, barely visible in the dim light of the moon. "I don't believe this." Annie picked up the lock and pulled the rounded shackle to confirm that it was locked. "I am positive that I put this lock on the door correctly before I locked it." She pulled the door open to reveal the bucket of fishing rods and the charcoal sitting inside, but no lighter fluid.

Her stomach churned. She was certain that she'd locked the door correctly. There simply was no way that both she and Frank would have missed the lock falling to the ground right before their eyes. Someone had to have removed the lock again later, but to do that, they'd need the key, which Annie kept in her office, except when she happened to keep it in her pocket. Annie tried to remember whether or not she'd seen the shed key when she'd emptied her pockets at bedtime, but she honestly couldn't recall if she'd seen it or not.

Rory put a hand on Annie's shoulder. "Annie, you don't think Devon would have--"

"Would have what? Set fire to the deck he helped you build?" Anger tainted her tone. "You know he wouldn't do that."

"I'm sorry. I know you're right. I just--I don't see who else would have known the lighter fluid was even in there."

Annie groaned. "Frank knew. I showed him the fishing rods this evening, during dinner. I told him you could show him our favorite fishing spot."

Rory thought this over, then shook his head. "I don't know, he doesn't strike me as the kind of person who would do this."

"Did you see anyone, Rory?" Bessie had made her way to the shed, picking her way carefully through the darkness. "How did you know to come out here?"

"I had my window open," he replied. "I smelled smoke and thought my camper was on fire. It took me a minute to realize that the smell was coming from down behind the house. I didn't think, just grabbed a bucket from the back of my truck and legged it."

"Well, we're sure glad you did," Bessie assured him. "Is it out good and proper?"

"I think so," he replied, moving back towards the deck. "We'd be able to see any sparks still glowing, so I think it's good," he answered again, trying to reassure the two women. "I'll be able to see the damage better in the morning. I guess it must have got one of the lights, knocked them all out," he continued. Something caught his eye. "Wait a minute," he said, moving past Bessie and kneeling on the deck. He reached for something Annie couldn't see, then an instant later the deck was awash in light.

95

"Somebody unplugged those lights." Annie had a terrible feeling in her gut. "I'm guessing whoever it was that tried to burn my deck down didn't want to be seen," she said, gritting her teeth.

"Well, why on earth would somebody try to burn down our deck? It just makes no sense!" Bessie put her fingertips to her temples. "Whoever did this needs to pay for the damage, that's for sure." She *hmmphed* and *hawwed* a little, then sighed. "I'm going back to bed. My body thinks it should be drinking coffee and my brain knows it's supposed to be under the covers. I'll see y'all in the morning." She didn't wait for a response, but turned and made her way back up to the house.

"She's really mad," Rory noted. "I've never seen your mother lost for words before."

Annie shook her head. "She's not the only one. Rory, thank god you woke up when you did. I'd hate to think what would have happened…" She let her words trail off. "What time is it, anyway?"

Rory glanced at his watch. The luminous dial glowed gently in the darkness. "A little past one. You'd better go get some sleep."

She started to protest, but Rory shushed her gently. "No, go on. Whoever did this wouldn't be stupid enough to come back out here now. If it was one of your guests, you'll figure it out. If it was someone else, well, we'll deal with that tomorrow, after you get a good night's sleep." He put his arm around her shoulder and gave her a half-hug. Annie felt a combination of relief, despair, and the sudden realization that she was standing in the middle of her backyard, wrapped up in Rory's arm and wearing a pair of fairly threadbare pajamas. She pulled away from him with a sigh.

"Goodnight, Rory. I'll see you first thing in the morning. We can assess the damage then, I guess." Reluctantly, Annie made her way back up to the house. She couldn't shake the feeling that someone was watching her the entire way, but when she turned to look, Rory was nowhere to be seen. Somewhere in the silence of the evening, she was sure she heard a bird calling out, and from the corner of her eye she could just make out the flutter of a blood red wing flying away off into the darkness.

13

Fishing For Information

Annie's eyelids fluttered open for the second time since she'd gone to sleep and found her mother again, though, thankfully, this time she was fully dressed and carrying coffee. "I thought you might like a cup before you had to come downstairs and deal with our guests," she explained. "Truthfully, I wasn't expecting all of them to be up so early, but I had barely even poured my first cup of coffee and wouldn't you know that Marie woman was standing right there in the kitchen behind me, creeping around like some sort of ghost."

Annie sat up and saw that her mother had brought two cups of coffee. "I'll just drink this up here and then we can go down and sort out breakfast."

"Mama, that's not like you. You're normally the life of the party, the friendliest gal in the room. What's got you so riled up? Is it the fire?" She took her coffee from Bessie and put it to her lips, inhaling the sweet, rich scent before taking a sip. It was perfect, two sugars and cream, and she'd need lots of it if she wanted to make it through the day. Sleep had eluded her for a while after she'd returned to bed, and once she finally fell into a slumber, it was wrought with nightmare images of flames and her dead husband's coffin.

"Oh, I don't know," Bessie admitted. "I just feel like my nerves are on edge. Ever since that fella drowned in the pond, I just can't help but think that this place really is cursed."

Annie groaned. "No, Mama, not you, too! Listen, that man didn't drown. You know that Emmett thinks he was killed by somebody he double-crossed or conned out of some money. That sort of thing could happen absolutely anywhere."

"Yes, but it happened here," Bessie countered, "and that Anderson woman was killed here--"

"By her greedy, deranged fiance," Annie said, "which was unfortunate but again, had nothing to do with any sort of curse. If you ask me, it says more about the state of the world today than it does about this place." Annie finished her coffee and sat the cup on the bedside table. "I'm going to jump in the shower. You can hide in here from some made-up curse if you want, or you can go downstairs and start breakfast. Personally, I'm starving, and I'm sure Rory would love a cup of coffee."

Annie's guilt-trip worked beautifully. "Fine," Bessie huffed, "but if you find my dead body down there--"

"I'll bury you up on the hill next to Rose," Annie joked.

Bessie looked as though she might say something more or at least spit out a snappy comeback, but she simply shook her head and left the bedroom, carrying Annie's empty mug with her.

By the time Annie made her way downstairs, Bessie was her usual, cheerful self, albeit a little more quiet than usual. Since breakfast wasn't usually served until a little later, Annie suggested that the guests take coffee out on the front porch.

"It will give me a chance to sort out the fishing rods, too," she explained. Frank was eager to embark on his fishing trip and Rob had decided to join them. Annie was amused, but not shocked when Kizzy announced that she'd love to go with the men. She assured Frank that she could handle a fishing rod as well as he could, though she seemed slightly squeamish when the topic of bait was brought up.

Rory volunteered to lead the group to Annie's favorite fishing spot on the far side of the pond. He agreed that it was the best spot for catching fish, though it was quite a trek and very secluded.

"You'll need to watch out for snakes," he advised while checking the rods and tackle box. "And check yourselves for ticks afterward."

Kizzy laughed when Frank asked, "You meant that's not just a cute country music song?"

Bessie and Doris busied themselves in the kitchen, preparing a picnic lunch for the intrepid fishers. They prepared sandwiches and thermoses filled with tea, then piled in leftover pie from the night before. "That will curb my temptation to pick at it," Doris laughed, closing up the basket.

As the small group headed out behind the house, there was a collective gasp as they approached the deck.

"Oh, my gosh, what happened out here?" Kizzy asked, pointing towards the deck with her rod.

"Looks like a fire," Frank suggested. "Must have happened last night," he added.

Rob stayed silent. Rory told them that there had been a small fire, but he'd put it out before it spread.

"Oh, my goodness--it's lucky you caught that," Kizzy exclaimed. "That whole deck could have gone up in flames!"

Rory cringed at the thought and changed the subject. "I would normally take the boat out, but it only holds two people, so I'm afraid we're going to have to hoof it," he joked. It's not too far, but it will help you work up an appetite getting there. Do any of you have a cell phone?"

Rob nodded. "I do."

"Good. I'm going to leave you all over there and come back here. I've got some work to do this morning," he said simply. "Just call me or Annie and I'll come get you when you're finished if you don't think you can find your way back."

The guests laughed at this, but after traveling in and out of patches of trees, away from the bank of the pond and back towards it, they could see the sense in his suggestion. "There are parts of this place that are just so overgrown," Rory explained, "it's hard to go anywhere in a straight line. I'll get around to clearing it up--eventually."

After about twenty-five minutes of walking, they came to a stop. Rory pushed aside some branches of a prickly bush to reveal a stunning view of the pond. From where they were, the house was completely out of sight.

"How big is this pond?" Rob asked, impressed with the secluded spot.

"It runs along most of the property, I think. It's kind of narrow, for a pond, but it's a good size for fishing. Actually, this is the back of the property line for the bed-and-breakfast."

"Who owns the rest of that land?" Kizzy asked pointing to the trees behind them.

"I'm not sure," Rory admitted. "But whoever it is, I've never seen them. It's pretty secluded out here. Y'all make sure you stay together, don't go wandering around in the woods. I don't want to have to send out any search parties," he joked.

Rory felt only a little uneasy as he left the small group and made his way back to the house. Annie greeted him by the deck.

"Everything good with the fishermen?" she asked, thinking that she really ought to say 'fisherpeople,' but it didn't sound quite right.

"Yep. They should be fine as long as they don't try and wander off," he sighed. He reached over and brushed a coarse black hair off of Annie's shoulder. "That dog sleep alright last night?"

Annie looked down and realized that her shirt was speckled with dog fur from an early morning cuddle with the young dog. She hated to admit that she had already grown quite fond of the little guy and she secretly hoped that the veterinarian wouldn't find a microchip when they went to his office later that morning.

"Yep," she replied, "he even slept through our little incident," she added, gesturing to the deck. "I'm going to take Devon and the pup to see Dr. Fisher so we can make sure the dog doesn't already belong to someone. I guess I might need to stop and buy dog food, too, depending on what we find out." She picked at the fur on her shirt as she spoke and she knew that Rory could tell she was avoiding discussing the fire.

He simply nodded as she spoke, then replied, "While you're gone, I'll take care of the mess from our little 'incident.'" He looked around the backyard, surveying the place for any clues that they might have missed the night before. Annie could tell that he was uneasy about the fire--who wouldn't be? There was something extremely unsettling about waking up to a fire. It was bad enough that it was unexpected, but the fact that it appeared to have been deliberately set while everyone slept, that had Annie's nerves on edge, too.

"Thank you, Rory." She leaned in and hugged him. He smelled like soap and sweat, like fresh air and hard work. She sighed. "I don't know what I'd do without you," she said finally.

Rory smiled. "I guess you'd be leading the fishing expeditions," he joked. They separated and went off in different directions, both determined to get their jobs done as soon as possible.

Annie hated leaving Bessie alone to entertain the remaining guests, so she hurried along to Dr. Fisher's veterinary office. After confirming that the dog had no microchip, she and Devon detoured to visit Emmett at the police station.

They waited with the puppy in the lobby of the station while the receptionist called the Chief in his office. Soon, he appeared behind the glass partition that separated the lobby from the rest of the station.

"Well, now, what have we here?" Emmett's booming voice startled the pup, making it yelp. "Sorry, little fella," Emmett apologized to the dog, scratching behind its ear. "Didn't mean scare the little guy."

"This is the dog I told you about," Annie replied, stroking the pup's head. "Devon and Rory found him wandering along the road by my house. He was dirty and hungry, but the vet says he seems okay, though he needs to be wormed and vaccinated."

Emmett nodded, unperturbed by the revelation that the pup had parasites. "Most stray pups are wormy," he said. He looked at Devon. "Did he have a collar or one of those microchip things?"

"No, sir. The vet says he's probably about four months old. He looks like he's part German Shepherd, you know, like the kind of dogs used in K9 units. I'm thinking maybe somebody couldn't find a home for him and just dumped him," the teen added. "I don't see how anyone could be so cruel. Look at that face--those big old eyes!" Devon leaned in and let the dog lick his face. "But Mom says I can keep him, so it's all good, right little guy?"

The dog's tail wagged in excitement. "Chief, you said you found dog hair in the car? What color was it?" Something had been nagging Annie since the Chief's call the day before. She felt like she kept finding pieces to a puzzle, but had no idea how they all fit together.

"'Bout the same color as that," Emmett replied, pointing at the pup. "Wouldn't surprise me if your missing guest was planning on bringing a friend with him," he added.

"Do you mean that this pup was the dead guy's dog?" Devon asked. "No way!" He looked at the pup for a long moment. "Then it was fate that we found him," he added. "If Rory and I hadn't been driving along our road right then, he probably would have ended up getting hit or starving." He rubbed the dog's furry ears affectionately. "I know what your name is," he said confidently. "Your name is Karma because it was definitely fate that brought us together."

Annie stifled a giggle. "What?" Devon asked, a little hurt that his mother didn't understand the importance of the name.

"Nothing," she replied, "It's a great name. A little dramatic, but unique." She turned back to Emmett. "Do you need the dog for your investigation?" she asked, wondering to herself how she would tear Devon and the pup apart if he did.

"Nope. I think we'll just go on the assumption that Karma here got separated from the deceased at some point. I don't know if that has any bearing on the man's death, but I don't see any harm in you guys taking this little fellow home and fattening him up." He pulled Annie to the side, then added, "I understand y'all had a fire at your place last night?"

Annie was baffled. "How did you know?"

"Your mama called me this morning, first thing. She said you wouldn't want to worry me, but I'll just say what I've been saying-- be careful."

"It was on the deck, nowhere near the house," she replied as if it would make the whole situation less bad.

"You want me to send somebody out there? Dust for prints, maybe call in an arson investigator?"

Annie shook her head quickly. "No, I just want to get through this week and send these guests on their way. If the killer is found before then, all the better," she added, hoping Emmett would reassure her that his officers had a lead on the killer already.

"I'm sure we'll sniff them out in no time," he reassured her. "In the meantime, you've got yourself a great little guard dog here," he said, patting Karma on the head. "And you know what they say?"

Annie looked puzzled. "What do they say?"

Emmett grinned. "Well, you know that people who do bad things have to deal with Karma, right?"

The dog let out a little bark, and Annie laughed. "Well, I feel a lot better now," she replied. "I'll just let Karma here handle all my problems. I'm sure he'll sniff out the culprit in no time."

As they headed back to the car, Annie couldn't help but wonder if maybe fate really had put the little dog in Rory and Devon's path. It seemed like a lucky coincidence that they'd found the little guy. "Karma, it's a shame you can't speak," she whispered to the dog as she rubbed its head. "You might be able to tell us who killed your owner."

Karma looked at her with big brown eyes and barked in apology. Annie sighed, and drove them all home.

14

Tired and Sick

It was already getting hot when Annie arrived back home a little after ten in the morning. They'd made good time on their errands, even after stopping at the MegaMart for dog food. She'd also insisted on getting the pup a collar and soft little bed. "You won't want him sleeping with when you realize how much he sheds," she advised her son. While Devon took Karma up to his room, Annie sought out her mother.

Bessie was sitting out on the screened-in porch of the rear veranda. Doris sat with her, a tray filled with a teapot, cups, and accessories sat between them on a table.They were chatting quietly, watching Rory work on the deck, and didn't hear Annie approach.

"I had a feeling I'd find you two out here," Annie teased them, causing Bessie to startle slightly. "Didn't mean to make you jump, Mama. What are you two plotting out here?"

Bessie looked slightly red-faced. "Oh, nothing," she said quickly. "We were just swapping recipes," she insisted.

"And drinking tea," Doris confirmed, lifting a china cup for emphasis. Both women fell immediately silent and took to sipping their teas noisily.

"Well, okay, then," Annie replied in an exaggerated voice. She got the distinct impression that the two women had just been talking about her before she walked up, though she had no idea why her mother wouldn't include her in the conversation. Annie's life was, for the most part, an open book. She saw Doris look intently at Rory, then over at Annie, as though she was comparing the two. Annie's own cheeks reddened as she realized that they must have been talking about her relationship with Rory.

"Dr. Fisher says the dog doesn't have a microchip," Annie said, and it came out a little louder than she'd intended. "And he's healthy, apart from being slightly wormy," she added more quietly.

"Most puppies are wormy," Bessie replied cheerfully. "So we have a new dog!" She sat her cup on the table and gestured towards an empty one, pointing at Annie to ask if she wanted a cup.

Annie shook her head 'no.' "Devon's named him already," she laughed. "He calls him Karma. I told him it was a little dramatic, but I guess that under the circumstances, he's got a pretty dramatic origin story. I stopped by Emmett's place," she added, trying to be discreet in front of her guest. "He has an interesting theory he wanted to share," she added.

"You mean he thinks the dog belonged to the dead man?" Bessie picked up her tea once again and peered over the rim of the cup. "He called me after you left. I think he's fishing for an invite to supper on Sunday. Ever since I told him I'm making chicken and dressing he's been pestering me non-stop," she said, a giggle coloring her voice.

Annie was annoyed at her mother for discussing what she considered sensitive police investigation information in front of

Doris, but the Ohio woman simply shook her head and cupped her hands around her tea. "I hope they catch whoever killed that man. He might have been a criminal, but nobody deserves to end up like he did." She shook her head. "And now all his victims will never get a chance to get their money back," she added. "It's not like you can get money from a dead man, is it?"

Bessie agreed. "It's an awful situation all round, isn't it? But let's not talk about such depressing things right now." She patted Doris's arm gently. "Would you like to see my favorite recipe for pineapple upside down cake? It's an old one, been in my family for years, but it makes the best dessert!"

Annie left the two women discussing cakes and cookies. She went back inside the house and headed for the kitchen, where she stopped to make herself a cup of coffee. She reached into the cupboard and pulled out a tin filled with single-serve coffee pods. Her mother may prefer old-fashioned coffee from a coffee pot, but Annie was unashamedly in love with her Keurig, and she breathed a sigh of relief when the aroma of French vanilla coffee filled the kitchen and her blue ceramic mug.

Annie added her cream and sugar, then took a long drink, still holding the spoon that she'd used to stir the drink. Setting the mug on the counter, she reached for the faucet to rinse the spoon in the sink when something odd caught her eye. A pointed piece of clear plastic sat wedged up against the tap. Annie picked it up and examined it. It appeared to be some sort of a lid, though she had no idea what it fit. She was just about to toss it in the trash when Rory came into the kitchen through the back door. Annie slipped the lid into her back pocket absentmindedly and turned to Rory.

"Annie, I thought you should know that I'm going to go get your guests from the far side of the pond," he said, catching his breath just a little. "Rob just called me and said he's sick. Actually, he said Kizzy's sick, too. I'm not sure about Frank, but Rob sounded kind of shaken up." He paused for a moment. "I'll try to be as quick as I can, and I've got my phone if you need me."

Annie could tell Rory was anxious about something. It crossed her mind that he didn't want to leave her alone after the murder and the fire, but Annie knew she could take care of herself. "Go, don't worry about me, for heaven's sake. Did Rob say how sick he was? Is he like, puking sick?"

Rory shrugged. "I don't know, but he doesn't seem like the kind of guy to fuss over a little indigestion. They might have picked up a nasty stomach bug, you just never know what they got up to before coming here," he added.

Annie frowned. It seemed awfully strange that only Rob and Kizzy would be affected by some unexplained illness. Still, she suspected that maybe Rob had exaggerated his illness in order to come back to the house sooner. She doubted that the younger guests had much in common with Frank, and with the temperature already in the upper eighties, they were all probably getting tired of the heat.

"Thanks for letting me know. You go on and get them, I'll go see if I can round up some antacids and Pepto. I never realized that running a bed-and-breakfast required nursing skills," she joked.

Annie stepped out the back door and watched Rory walk away until he disappeared in the tree line. She turned and went back into the kitchen, debating whether she should say anything to her mother, who would undoubtedly kick up a fuss over the sick guests. Annie decided to wait until Rory and the others returned before she said anything. She wouldn't want Doris to worry, and Bessie would almost certainly say something to the woman.

Annie walked across the kitchen and opened the door that led down into the cellar. It was dark and cool down there, and it happened to be the perfect place to stash emergency supplies. She flipped a switch and a single bare bulb burst into light, casting a yellow glow on rows of canned foods, her mother's gardening supplies, and an assortment of items that they had yet to find permanent homes for.

Across the room was a sturdy metal shelving unit filled with clear plastic tubs. Annie walked over to it and pulled out a tub labeled "medical stuff." She vaguely remembered putting a few bottles of antacids in the tub just a few weeks before when she'd stocked up during a sale at the MegaMart.

"It's always smart to keep these on hand," her mother had advised. "These and Band-Aids, you can never have too many."

Annie noticed that the door to the breaker box was slightly ajar. Although it was brand new, the door didn't want to stay shut for some reason. Despite Rory's best efforts, the door always managed to pop open, which wasn't strictly a problem, but it drove Annie crazy. She couldn't stand a slightly open door. She'd lost count of the number of times she'd scolded Devon for leaving cabinets open in the kitchen and her own mother for leaving doors ajar around the house. Either push it completely shut or leave it wide open, but a door that was slightly ajar aggravated her to no end.

She reached up and pushed the door closed, only to have it pop open again. She tried again, wiggling the catch until she thought it might just stay in place, but as she pulled her hand away she was rewarded with a 'click' and the door popping back out of place. Frustrated, she pushed the door closed and pounded the catch with her fist. It finally gave in and stayed where she wanted it to, but she didn't have a chance to gloat.

"You can hit it all you want, but I don't think that it will help."

Annie jumped, turning so quickly that she knocked the bottle of antacids off onto the floor.

"I didn't mean to startle you," Marie apologized, "but I saw this door open and just wondered where it led. I always say that an open door is an invitation to the spirit world."

Annie picked up the antacids and put them in her back pocket. They fit snugly, digging into her tailbone and stretching against the fabric of her capris. "You gave me a fright," Annie admitted. "I didn't hear you come down the stairs."

Marie didn't respond. She simply smiled and looked around the room, studying her surroundings. "Is this the cellar?" she asked after a moment. Annie nodded. "These old homes have such character, don't you think?"

Annie thought the cellar was fairly boring. It was cooler down here, which was its only benefit, as far as she was concerned. The room felt clammy to her, and with no windows, it felt claustrophobic, despite the fact that it was nearly as large as her kitchen.

"We don't encourage guests to come down here," Annie responded, annoyed that Marie had frightened her and didn't seem the least bit remorseful about it. Her apology sounded insincere, and that bit about the spirit world rubbed Annie the wrong way. She was sick of Marie's references to ghosts and spirits, and Annie found herself looking forward to Marie's checkout date with some small amount of glee.

Marie studied Annie for a moment. "You look like you've lost someone recently. No," she amended, "not recently, but you have been thinking about him recently. Your father," she added, "is that correct?"

Annie squinted in the low light. "My father died five years ago.

I do think of him often, yes, and I'm sure he's been on my mind in the past few days." She pointed towards the stairs, motioning for Marie to make a move.

Marie nodded and began to walk very slowly up the bare wooden steps. "I believe he thinks of you, too," she replied, exiting the cellar ahead of Annie. The two women stood in the middle of Annie's kitchen for a long moment. The house was silent around them, save for the creaking of the floor as Annie shifted her weight from one foot to the other.

Finally, Marie broke the silence. "You don't believe in what I do." It was a statement, a challenge.

"I'm sure that you believe in it," Annie began, "but I've always been a little skeptical. I've never had any sort of experience that would make me think that there's any way for those who've died to communicate with us." She kept her tone light and polite, trying not to offend her houseguest. Annie thought very briefly of the redbird she'd seen the morning that she'd found Lou's body. Did she believe in some sort of afterlife where the dead could visit the living? Her head told her no, but her heart wanted very badly to think that there was a way she might be able to speak to her father again.

With a small shudder, Annie realized that this was probably how Lou Ross had operated. Maybe not by tricking people into believing that he could commune with spirits, but by preying on the things their hearts wanted most, convincing them to ignore the sound judgments that their brains tried to make, and twisting their desires against them, separating his victims from their money by lying to them about how he could give them what they most wanted.

Annie took a deep breath. "Miss Robichaud, can I help you with anything?"

Marie smiled again, the same vapid smile that she always seemed to have pasted on her face. Annie couldn't help but wonder if the woman was on some sort of drug. She tried to discreetly sniff the air for telltale signs that the woman may have been smoking something. She got a distinctive whiff of cinnamon and patchouli, and a slight hint of something earthy and mellow, nothing too sketchy.

"I actually came to ask if it would be alright if I lit some incense and did a small smudging ritual, you know, to clear the air?"

Annie wrinkled her eyebrows in confusion. "What's wrong with the air? Is it your room--I'm sorry, that musty smell is just part of the house. I can get you some air freshener if that would help."

"Smudging is simply a cleansing ritual to remove bad karma and bless a space," Marie explained. "It's very simple, and there's not nearly as much smoke as you'd think."

Annie's mouth made a small 'o', then closed again. "You mean sage burning, don't you?" Marie nodded enthusiastically. "Well, I don't mind if you do it in your own room, as long as there's no risk of fire. I'd rather you didn't burn incense, though. I'd be afraid that the cat might find her way into your room and knock it over. One fire is quite enough for one week," she added, trying to make light of the fire from the night before.

"Well, yes, I could see how you'd be nervous about that," Marie agreed. "If you change your mind and would like for me to use my sage in any other parts of the house, or down by the pond--"

Annie put a hand up, cutting her off. "I'll let you know if I change my mind."

Marie smiled again and turned to wander off towards the sitting room. Annie rubbed her temples and pulled the bottle of antacids from her pocket. Something fell out of her pocket and hit the floor, skittering to a stop by her foot. She bent to retrieve the small plastic lid that she'd found earlier, having forgotten completely that it had been in her pocket all along. She moved to toss the errant bit of plastic into the garbage but decided to keep it instead. She didn't want to find the bottle it belonged to later and regret tossing the little lid, so she sat it on the windowsill above the sink.

Annie rinsed out her coffee cup from earlier and wiped down the counter, then struggled to decide what she should do next. She knew that there was likely to be a million things that needed to be done, from cleaning the house to preparing the food that would be cooked later for supper, but all she really wanted to do was lie down and take a nap. Knowing that this was a bad idea (she'd probably sleep like the dead and wake up feeling miserable,) she settled on going to find Devon and making sure that Karma hadn't destroyed her son's room the night before.

As she started up the stairs, Annie was greeted by the sound of someone calling her name. "Mrs. Richards, do you have a minute?"

Annie cringed inwardly as Alexander George approached and stopped just inches from her face. "I'm sorry to bother you, but can you see my eyes? Are they terribly red?"

Annie looked at the man's watery eyes, which were slightly red, but not alarmingly so. "They do look a little irritated," she conceded.

"I'm not surprised. I can't find my eyedrops anywhere, and that cat has been all over my bed, I just know it. I found a hair on my pillow," he declared, "and I'm sure it's the same color as the feline."

He held a hair that was far too long to belong to the cat. "I believe that's a human hair," she replied, "but I'll be happy to wash your bedding for you. I'm not sure how the cat would have gotten into your room--you do keep your door closed when you leave?"

He looked at her as though she'd just begun speaking a foreign language. "Of course, I do. I have a method," he continued. "I close the door, then I test the knob to make sure it's locked, then I unlock the door to make sure my key still works, and then I close it up again and wiggle it again, to make sure it's locked." He rubbed at his eyes. "It's a very sound method," he added.

Annie was beginning to realize that Alexander George was far stranger than she'd first believed. His compulsive behavior would have been amusing if he hadn't been so pitiful standing there with his weepy eyes.

"What type of eyedrops do you use? I may have some downstairs in my medicine cabinet that you could use."

"Oh, no," he replied. "I couldn't use yours. You should never share medications," he explained. "Do you think I could ask that Rory fellow to drive me to the pharmacy to buy some more?"

"Rory's gone to collect Mr. Martin, Miss Fitzsimmons, and Mr. Reynolds from their fishing trip, but I'm sure he wouldn't mind helping you as soon as he comes back." She gestured to his room. "Would you like me to change the bedding for you in the meantime?"

Alexander shook his head. "No, I already put on a clean set of sheets. I always travel with a spare, just in case," he stated, as though this was something everyone did. "And I'm not angry at the cat, just so you know. But, I would love to know how the clever little creature managed to get into my locked bedroom, that's for sure." He laughed heartily, as though he'd just told the world's funniest joke. "Oh, can you imagine her standing on her little furry paws, picking the lock!" He stood there for a moment, lost in his own thoughts, then he spoke again. "Thank you for helping me, Mrs. Richards. I think I'll just go and wait in the sitting room until Rory comes back." He didn't wait for her to respond, but strode down the stairs and turned to head into the sitting room.

Exasperated at the strange exchange, Annie headed down the hallway. At least there were no more guests left upstairs who could complain to her or ask her crazy questions. She let out a long, loud sigh in defiance of her responsibilities, and hoped that Karma wouldn't have another mess for her to clean up.

15

A Dead Man's Forwarding Address

"I think I'm going to be sick again." Kizzy hugged the bowl that Bessie had given her and pulled her knees up to her chest. Her face was pale and a fine sheen of sweat had broken out on her forehead.

"Are you sure you don't want me to call our local doctor's office?" Annie asked, not for the first time.

Kizzy looked at Rob, who was in a similar state, hugging his own bowl. He closed his eyes for a moment, then responded. "I don't see what a doctor could do that Bessie's not already doing," he answered. Bessie had given them both a dose of activated charcoal, just in case their sickness was caused by something that they'd eaten. Annie chided her mother for playing doctor and possibly taking risks with their guests' health, but neither Rob nor Kizzy seemed worse for having taken it. In fact, they had both perked up considerably since they'd arrived back at the house.

Despite Kizzy's announcement, she wasn't sick, and within a few hours of returning from the pond, both houseguests were feeling well enough to nibble saltine crackers and sip ginger ale. Bessie fluttered nearby most of the time, fussing over the two just as if they were her own children.

Annie quizzed Rob about his illness, hoping to figure out why he and Kizzy had become so sick when Frank was absolutely fine. "Did you all eat anything different from everyone else this morning?"

Rob shook his head. "Not that I know of. I had toast, I think Kizzy had the same thing, and we all drank the tea that Bessie put in the thermos for us."

"Uh, no, actually that's not true," Frank chimed in. "I had water. Brought a bottle for each of us, but I'm the only one who drank mine."

Bessie's face went white. "Oh, no--do you think the tea was bad?"

"I've never gotten sick from drinking bad tea before," Rob assured her, "and in any case, it tasted just fine." He took a small sip of his ginger ale. "You know, I haven't been that sick since college," he said. "My roommate decided it would be fun to spike my beer with Visine," he continued.

"Visine eyedrops?" Bessie asked, shaking her head. "Oh, how awful! It's a wonder he didn't kill you," she exclaimed.

"Oh, I don't think it would have killed me," Rob assured her, "but it made me as sick as a dog for a day or so. Of course, I didn't have someone to look after me and give me charcoal," he said, smiling at the woman. "You remind me so much of my grandmother. She was always coming up with these home remedies that sounded crazy, but they always seemed to work."

Bessie returned his smile with one of her own. "Sometimes, the old ways are the best," she replied.

Annie rolled her eyes. She knew for a fact that her mother had only bought those charcoal tablets over the summer after she'd taken an interest in holistic medicine. But to hear Bessie talk,

Annie would swear the woman thought of herself as some sort of granny witch or medicine woman.

Bessie excused herself to go to the kitchen and Doris followed, chatting away with Bessie about herbs and teas. Frank excused himself, too, opting for a nap after his fishing adventure. Annie envied him. She was feeling the effects of her lack of sleep more than ever and debating another cup of coffee when Rob touched her arm.

"Annie, I don't want to alarm you, but I think somebody put something in our tea."

Annie sat up straight in her chair. "What?"

"Shhh," he whispered, "let's keep this between us for now. I believe that someone put something in the flask of tea that Kizzy and I drank from, something to make us really sick."

Annie glanced over at Kizzy, who had her eyes closed. "Who? Why? Rob, why would someone want to hurt you and Kizzy?" Annie's mind turned the situation over and over in her head. Three guests went out, two got sick. Frank had conveniently avoided the tea, and he'd been sniffing around the deck the evening before the fire. Then there was his angry outburst about the dead man in her pond--she suddenly felt sick herself.

Rob shook his head. "I don't know. And I'm not sure why someone would want me sick, maybe even sick enough to leave this place."

"Maybe even dead?" Annie's voice cracked as she spoke quietly. "What if someone was trying to poison you?"

Rob looked thoughtful. "I want to send the tea to Emmett to see if he can have it tested. If there's something in there, maybe we can figure out who tampered with the tea."

Annie nodded. "I'm sure Emmett could tell us if there's something in the tea. I'll take it over there right away." Annie made a move to rise from the chair, but Rob stopped her.

"I could be wrong, and this could be just a fluke, some sort of bug or bad food, but I have a real hunch that someone tried to make me very sick, and I want to know why. Let's keep this quiet for now, if you don't mind."

Annie nodded. "I'll be discreet. You just keep an eye out for any other suspicious activities." She hesitated, then added, "Why do you think Frank avoided the tea?"

Rob laughed. "Because Kizzy wouldn't put the thermos down. And I don't think he's much of a tea drinker. I guess that's just lucky for him," he finished.

Yeah, very lucky, indeed. Annie rose from her chair and headed straight for the kitchen. If she knew her mother, there was a chance that the picnic basket had already been emptied and the dishes washed. She only hoped that she wasn't too late to get the thermos filled with tea so she could pay Emmett yet another visit. This time, at least, she didn't have a dead body to go along with the tea, and for that, she was very grateful.

A postcard in the mailbox notified Annie that she had a package waiting at the post office. She sorted through the rest of the mail quickly, tossed a few junk circulars, and piled the rest on the dashboard of her truck. Rory sat in the passenger seat, sweating as he waited for the AC to kick in. "Gotta run by the post office to pick up a package," she told him. "You mind if we do that first?"

Rory shook his head. "You're driving. We could go wherever you want," he replied, a tired grin creeping onto his lips. "How about we grab us a cold drink while we're out? As long as it's not tea," he joked, shaking the thermos of tea he held in his lap.

"Thanks for riding with me to see Emmett." Annie turned out of her driveway and onto the road. She could see the heat shimmering above the asphalt and hear the gentle thump of her tires against the road as they headed towards town. "I know you have a million things to do back at the house--"

Rory laughed. "Like I'd get anything done in this heat. Besides, your guests keep asking me questions, and that's not really my thing."

Annie was curious. "What kinds of questions?"

"Well, that Alexander fellow keeps asking me all kinds of questions about the history of the house, who built which part and when. He's a strange fellow, isn't he?" Annie nodded. "I think he might be one of those savants, you know. That man is like a walking encyclopedia when it comes to old houses. He was telling me all about the types of wood they used in the seventeen-hundreds, what kinds of tools they used, all sorts of stuff."

Annie glanced at Rory to see if he was joking. "Really? Wow, he's hardly said ten words to me," she replied. "And he is definitely strange. But, I guess if he was some sort of savant, it might explain his odd social behavior."

Rory continued. "That psychic lady rubs me the wrong way." Annie laughed, and Rory corrected himself. "I mean, she just grates on my nerves. All this 'the spirits are restless' crap--and I'm not the only one who doesn't care for her," he confided.

"I know, Devon told me she irritates him, too."

"No, not Devon. The dog."

Annie laughed. "Karma doesn't like her? It's probably because she smells like potpourri," she added, thinking to herself that the woman could use a good wash.

"I don't know what it is, but that pup likes everyone except Marie. I tend to trust dogs' opinions of people, and your dog has been pretty clear. He barks at her like crazy every time she gets near him."

"Rory, you can't just mistrust someone because the dog barks at them. Maybe she looks like someone he used to know. I doubt very seriously that Karma would have any reason to dislike Marie; it's not like she's done anything to him." Annie turned onto Main Street and drove on past the police station, then took a right onto the road that led to the post office.

She found a parking spot and parked the truck. Rory pointed across the street to a small convenience store. "How about I run over there and grab us a couple of cokes while you get your mail?"

"Make mine a diet coke, and you've got a deal." Annie gave Rory a little wink. "Gotta keep my girlish figure," she added with just a hint of sarcasm, patting her slightly rounded tummy. She'd gained nearly ten pounds since she'd moved back to Coopersville, but weight loss was the last thing on her mind. What with starting a new business, solving murders, and keeping her mother out of trouble, Annie had better things to do than worry about a few extra pounds.

"You need a diet coke like I need another hole in my head, woman." Rory headed across the street, and five minutes later he was back, cold drinks in hand.

Annie had breezed into the post office and back out again in record time. She was surprised to find not one, but two, plain brown packages waiting for her inside. The clerk just shrugged and passed them over, barely glancing at Annie's driver's license as he compared the signatures when she signed to collect them. She was back in the truck before Rory, shaking the boxes gently and debating whether she should open them there or wait until she got back home.

"You going to open it?" Rory twisted open his soft drink slowly, letting the slow hiss of carbonation punctuate his question.

"Nah," she decided finally. "It's probably the back to school stuff I ordered for Devon. It can wait until we get back to the house.." She passed the boxes to Rory and took her own drink. It was cold and soothing, just what she needed.

Rory examined the smaller of the two packages. It was about the length and width of a textbook. "It's heavy," he noted. "I wouldn't want to be a student these days, that's for sure." He settled the packages on the floor beside his feet. "Didn't you say that the dead guy was having a package delivered to the house?" His question caught Annie off-guard. "What are you going to do with *that* package?" he asked.

"Take it to Emmett, I guess," Annie replied. "He'll know what to do with it. After all, it's not like Mr. Ross left any forwarding address."

Rory shrugged in agreement. "I guess you're right," he replied. "Unless you want to toss it in the pond, you know, his last known address."

Annie groaned. "That's totally not funny," she shot back. "I bet the address he gave me when he booked was a fake one," she mused. "Probably the credit card was bogus, too. Sheesh, I never thought about having to worry about this kind of stuff when I first thought about opening a bed-and-breakfast."

"You're doing a fine job," Rory reassured her. "You just got unlucky with this guy. Actually, come to think of it, he was pretty unlucky, too. I mean, he was probably looking forward to a nice relaxing stay, time off from cheating people out of their money, and look where he ended up. I guess karma caught up with him, huh?"

Annie sniffed. "Karma got away from him, now he's shedding all over my son's bed," she joked.

They pulled into the parking lot behind the police station and stepped out of the car. A low rumble sounded in the distance.

"Sounds like we might just get a storm," Rory noted.

Annie looked up at the still blue sky. "It doesn't look like rain," she argued, remembering back to another visit she'd made to the police station to get Rory out of jail when he'd been wrongly accused of killing a woman. It had rained that day, too, and she'd had to rush home to close all the windows in the house before the water could get in and cause damage.

If it did rain, she thought, at least her windows were closed today.

They entered the front lobby of the little brick police station. Myra Sedge sat behind the desk as always, her black hair in neat little braids and her uniform starched and pressed. "Oh, hey, there, Miss Annie," she greeted them. "You just can't stay away from this place, huh?"

Annie smiled back at the young woman. "I guess not. Is Emmett here?"

Myra nodded. "I'll call him for you. He was down in the holding area with Delbert and a couple of the other officers a little while ago. Let me see if I can get him for you."

Myra picked up a black phone receiver and pushed some buttons. Annie and Rory sat on a wooden bench that sat along the far wall. "Bring back memories?" Annie teased him. At the time that he'd been mistakenly arrested for killing Suzy Anderson, Annie definitely hadn't been in the mood for joking. Thankfully, Rory had put it behind him and had even made up with the Chief of Police, Emmett Barnes.

It was hard not to like Emmett. He was a friendly man who loved to tell jokes, share stories, and fish, all things that just happened to appeal to most men in Coopersville. As the Chief of Police, he was clever and cautious, never rushing to conclusions when it came to his investigations. He was nearly seventy, but had no desire to retire, partly because his work kept him busy and being busy kept him young.

Emmett's wife had passed away several years ago, and although he flirted terribly with many elderly women in town, Annie knew he held a special place in his heart for her mother. Bessie and Emmett spent many Sundays together, bonding over a shared love of food and books. Annie liked the old man, so did Rory. In fact, she couldn't really think of anyone who didn't like Emmett, except for maybe the criminals that he locked up, and even then, many of them didn't hold a grudge against Emmett Barnes for doing his job.

"You just can't stay away from this place, can you?" Emmett's booming voice reminded Annie of Sam Elliott, and she jumped a little.

"Hey, Emmett. I guess not," she replied.

"Rory, you keeping this one in line?" Emmett teased and Annie could swear that she saw just the slightest hint of a blush creep along Rory's jaw.

"You know there's no telling Annie what to do," Rory replied with a grin.

"I hate to bother you, Emmett, but we've had some trouble up at my place. Again."

Emmett's face went slack. "You found another body?"

"No!" Annie replied, shaking her head for emphasis. "Nothing like that, but I think somebody tried to hurt a couple of my guests." She briefly explained Rob and Kizzy's sickness and told Emmett what Rob had said to her about his suspicions.

"So Rob thinks somebody tried to poison him?" Emmett twisted his bushy mustache, a habit he had whenever he was thinking hard about something. "You got any proof?"

Annie held up the thermos and sloshed it around. "Here's what's left of the tea they drank. It's the only thing they both had that Frank didn't, and he didn't get sick."

Emmett took the thermos, opened it, and sniffed. "I'll have to send this off to see if there's anything in it. Rob and Miss Fitzsimmons are okay?"

"They're fine, now," Annie confirmed. "But whatever they had, it had them pretty sick earlier." Annie glanced at her watch. It was only a little past four in the afternoon, but the day had seemed to stretch on forever.

"Well, you did the right thing. I always say it's best to trust your instincts, and if Rob's instincts tell him that there's something funny in this tea, it's better to be safe than sorry, especially with the things that have been going on up at your place."

Annie's cheeks flushed slightly. "I'm afraid my place is going to get the wrong kind of reputation," Annie worried.

Emmett smiled sympathetically at her. "Teething pains, Annie, that's all it is. None of your other guests seem to be too bothered by it all, so you must be doing something right." He leaned against the edge of the counter. "I understand y'all had a little incident this morning, something about a fire?"

"Mama's been on the phone with you already, huh?" Annie sighed. "It was a little fire. Rory put it out."

"You know how it got started?" he asked.

"No, to be honest, we don't. I had a can of charcoal fluid in my shed, and it wasn't there after we noticed the fire." Annie sighed. "I have no idea why someone would want to burn the deck unless they were trying to get rid of evidence."

Emmett nodded and rubbed the ends of his mustache. "Anything else weird happens, you call me. Don't wait for your mama to do it, just trust your gut, Annie. Your gut won't ever steer you wrong."

Rory cleared his throat. "Uh, Chief, have you found anything else out about the dead man? More specifically, was he murdered?"

Emmett sighed. "Coroner confirmed he died from anaphylactic shock. Specifically, there were traces of unrefined peanut oil all over the man's face and mouth. Unless he was suicidal, I'd say somebody slipped it into a drink, since he didn't appear to have eaten anything right before he died. So, unofficially, yes, I'm going with murder. But officially, I just don't have any firm suspects."

"What about Kizzy Fitzsimmons?" Rory asked. Annie scowled. "What? I'm going to ask, even if you like the woman."

"Well," Emmett answered, "we found her prints on the phone, and another set, but not the dead man's. I'm still waiting to see if we get a match on the second set of prints, but anybody could have touched her phone, so I don't hold out much hope on that being any help."

"She swore blind that she had her phone in her room when she went to bed," Annie interjected, "Do you think she lied about that?"

"You told me she'd been drinking," Emmett replied. "Who knows what she really remembers about that night."

Annie's mind went to Frank's odd behavior at dinner the night before. "Have you confirmed whether or not the Martins were connected to Lou Ross?"

Emmett shook his head. "My gut says they are, but the guys going through the evidence from Lou's car haven't confirmed it."

She thought about the crumpled piece of paper she'd found in her office. Who would have been interested in what Frank and Doris looked like? Lou Ross certainly would have been interested in them if he'd stolen their money only months before. Did he have an accomplice waiting for him, comparing his description of them to the actual guests staying at the house? Annie was beginning to believe that someone did know that Lou Ross was coming to the bed-and-breakfast. But was he killed by a partner in his crimes, or one of his rightfully angry victims?

"I wish we had all the pieces of this puzzle. My guests are going to start leaving in a few days, and my gut tells me that if we don't figure out who killed Lou Ross before then, we may never find out who did it."

She shifted her purse on her shoulder, signaling that she was ready to leave. "Please, call me when you find out what, if anything, is in that tea. In the meantime, I'm going to go home and try to keep my guests from dying."

Emmett patted Annie on the back as he walked her to the door, and though she normally would have found this to be a patronizing gesture, she didn't mind Emmett doing it. Somehow, it felt fatherly, and she knew that Emmett was as annoyed by the mess with the money as she was.

"You keep your eyes and ears open, Annie. We're going to figure out who's messing with your guests, and when we do, I'd venture to say we'll figure out who killed Lou Ross." He shook Rory's hand and saw them to the door, as though they were guests leaving his home instead of two worried people leaving after bringing him evidence of a crime.

"Tell your Mama I'm still waiting for an invitation to dinner on Sunday," he called after them, and Annie knew that he was well-aware that Emmett Barnes never needed an invitation to dinner, but she made a mental note to have her mother send him one, just the same.

16

Dark Horses, Dark Houses

The drive home was uneventful, except for the fact that Annie realized halfway home that she'd forgotten to go to the pharmacy for Mr. George. They turned around in a dusty driveway and headed back into town so Annie could get the drops and an extra-large bottle of acetaminophen. Since she'd bought the plantation, she'd had more headaches than she cared to admit. She supposed that was just part and parcel of being a business owner, and the price of a bottle of headache pills was a small enough price to pay for her troubles.

Once they were back on the road, Rory asked the question Annie had been trying to answer for the past two days. "So who do you think knew the dead guy, and do you think they killed him?"

Annie shook her head. "Honestly, I don't know. Nobody seems to have known him, or if they did, they're doing a great job of acting like they didn't."

"Kizzy's an actress," he noted. "And her phone was found at the crime scene."

Annie only hesitated for a moment. "I don't think it was her. She just seems, oh, I don't know--too ditzy. And she was sick, remember? Why would she poison herself? It doesn't make any sense."

"Who would you say had the most reason to want the man dead?" Rory cocked his head to one side, waiting on Annie's answer.

"I hate to say it, but Frank seems like the most likely person, in my opinion. I mean, he got so angry when we were talking about Lou at dinner the other night, and he was with me when I got the fishing rods out of the shed. He saw the charcoal lighter fluid, he knew it was there. And he was nosing around on the deck just before that, like he was looking for something." She tightened her grip on the steering wheel. "He didn't get sick, either. Isn't that a little convenient, don't you think?"

Rory thought this over. "He's also an old man, and I doubt very seriously that Lou Ross would have gone down quietly if one of his victims had confronted him. Nobody heard a thing the night Lou died, and Emmett says that he had an allergic reaction." Rory ticked off each point on his fingers. "I'd say that if Lou ate or drank something with peanut oil in it, he had to have been offered it by someone he knew and trusted. Would you trust somebody you'd scammed out of ten thousand dollars?"

They turned onto the road that would take them to Rosewood Place. "Then who? Mr. George? He's hardly spoken to anyone the whole time he's been at the house, and he's as timid as a mouse. But, could he be a dark horse?" Annie didn't really believe her own suggestion, but she wanted to know what Rory thought.

He laughed gently. "I don't think that dog would hunt," he replied. "He's pretty harmless, I'd venture. Actually, he's a nice guy. Did you know he's been coming out to the barn and chatting with Devon and me?"

Annie had no idea that the man had been spending time with

her son and Rory. "Well, I guess he is a dark horse, then, just not the kind I thought." She glanced up as a cloud passed over the sun, turning the sky an ominous shade of gray. Perhaps the thunder they'd heard was a warning. The sky definitely didn't look blue and welcoming now; it had shifted into something that looked angry and spiteful, threatening to open up and pour down its vengeance onto them at any moment.

"You think that reporter's on the up and up?" Rory's question surprised Annie.

"Rob? Emmett seems to trust him. And he got sick, remember?"

"He could be smart, luring us off track while he gets away with murder."

"Why would he kill Lou Ross? What's in it for him, besides possibly getting to report the crime on the evening news? A bit of a drastic career move, don't you think?"

"Well, that just leaves the psychic," Rory replied. "She can talk to dead people, so why hasn't she just asked the dead guy who killed him? Maybe she did the dirty deed," he said, making his voice go wobbly in a bad impersonation of a ghost.

"Maybe she's not really psychic," Annie shot back. "I mean, come on, do you really buy her 'I can talk to dead people' schtick? I thought you were smarter than that, Rory Jenkins."

"Now, I didn't say I believe Marie is the real deal, but I never discount what people think about themselves," he answered. "She seems thoroughly convinced that she can communicate with spirits. I don't sense that she's putting that on," he continued. "If she's a fraud, she's a darned good one."

Annie's driveway appeared just up ahead, and as she turned into it a crack of thunder made her jump. Rory let out a low whistle. "Whoo, that was close. Let's get inside before we need a rowboat to get there," he teased.

They made it up the hill just as the rain began, and they made it onto the front porch just as it began coming down in earnest. It was a late summer storm full of fury and power, and Annie knew it would pass quickly. She could feel the air around her changing, releasing the pressure and heat that had caused the storm in the first place. Summer storms were good, they cleared the air and brought relief from the heat, but she knew they could also be deadly.

As if on cue, lightning arced across the sky, flashing light that was too bright for her eyes. "Let's go inside and check on everybody. Hopefully, nobody's foolish enough to be out in this."

They went in through the front door and were greeted by Bessie, who sighed loudly when she greeted them. She carried a tray filled with cookies and a pitcher of lemonade. "I'm so glad you're back! I swear, I have been just run off my feet since you've been gone," she complained. "Not that I mind, especially since our guests have been unwell, but I'm just glad there's someone else who can answer all of their questions," she finished.

"Questions? What kind of questions?" Annie asked.

"Oh, you know, Mr. George wants to know what kind of wood the fireplace is made of, Frank wants to know what kind of fish are in the pond, and that Robichaud woman," Bessie said her name like it was something exotic, "just keeps asking about people who died in the house. She seems awfully interested in that sort of thing," Bessie finished.

Annie felt bad for her mother, but she knew that she brought it on herself. Bessie had a habit of starting conversations with anyone who would listen, and Annie had a feeling that many of her guests' questions had risen from prior conversations with her mother. She was slightly amused by the fact that Bessie the Chatterbox had finally gotten tired of all the chatter.

"I'll take over hostess duties," Annie assured her. "You go sit, take a break." She turned to Rory and passed him the two boxes she still carried from the car. "Would you mind sticking these in the office for me real quick?" He took the boxes and disappeared down the hallway leading to the office.

Annie took the tray from her mother and wandered into the sitting room. Frank and Marie looked up from a game of cards and greeted her warmly. "Look what the storm brought in!" Frank laughed. "Glad you guys got back before the weather took a turn. It's rough out there!"

Marie sat in a corner chair, reading a book. She looked up and over the top of the book, gave Annie a little smile, then returned to her reading. Alexander George sat on the opposite side of the room. He had a book about the history of Coopersville open on his lap and appeared to be studying a map of the county printed inside. There was a distinct lack of chatter, she noted. Her mother was a terrible one to exaggerate.

Annie sat the tray on a coffee table in the middle of the room. "Here's a little snack to keep you all from starving until dinner," she chirped. "Just let me know if y'all need anything else." She turned and started towards the door, then remembered Mr. George's eyedrops.

"Oops, I almost forgot." She pulled the drops from her pocket and approached Alexander, who eyed her warily until she held out the small bottle.

"Oh, thank you," he said, his cautious face breaking into a bright smile. "These are exactly what I needed! I still have no idea what happened to my other bottle," he apologized. "I do hope your little kitty didn't try to eat the bottle. They are not suitable for internal consumption," he added soberly.

Annie smiled, not sure how to respond. "I'm sure they'll turn up eventually," she reassured him, "but these should help in the meantime."

She turned to leave the room, aware that all eyes were on her. It dawned on her that she'd never seen Alexander speak to any of the other guests, and she realized that they must all find him just as odd as she did. Immediately she felt ashamed of herself. The man had been nothing but kind to her, so what if he was a little odd? Annie had no right to judge the man for keeping to himself. Shyness was not a crime, after all.

Annie found Rory and Bessie in the kitchen, eating cookies and drinking coffee. The smell of food filled the kitchen, and Annie realized that her mother had not one, but two slow cookers simmering away on the counter. She could just make out the tang of spaghetti sauce seeping out of one and a hint of beef coming out of the other.

"Vegetable beef stew will be ready shortly, spaghetti's done already. I just have to make the cornbread and cook up the pasta," Bessie offered before Annie could ask what they were having for dinner. "I don't see any reason why I should slave over a hot stove all day," she quipped when Annie nodded towards the slow cookers.

"Your mom's a smart woman," Rory said, popping an entire chocolate chip cookie into his mouth. "And she's a darned fine cook."

Annie dropped into a chair beside her mother and picked up her own cookie. "You're making me fat, Mama."

Bessie laughed. "I didn't just put that cookie in your mouth."

Annie grinned back at her mother around a bite of cookie. "I've missed this. You know, despite all the dead bodies that keep popping up in my life now, I am so glad that we bought this place. Daddy would have loved it," she added quietly.

Bessie nodded thoughtfully. "He would have."

Rory cleared his throat. "He was a good man, your daddy," he said to Annie. "Always treated me good, even though I was such a jerk to his little girl." Rory had dated Annie in high school, and they'd been steady and serious for nearly two years until Rory broke it off without explanation just after they'd graduated. Annie had eventually left for college, married, and moved to New York City. Now, all these years later, here they sat.

"He knew you were a good man, too, Rory," Bessie assured him.

"I'm glad you're here, too, Rory." Annie smiled at him. It had been hard at first, spending so much time with someone she'd once been so close to, someone who'd broken her heart. But as the summer passed, they fell into a comfortable friendship. She was a long way from being ready to ever think about dating again, her husband hadn't even been dead for a full year, and Rory's friendship was reassuring. Sure, she felt a few pangs of regret that they'd lost contact, and sometimes old memories would stir up uncomfortable feelings inside of her, but for the most part, their relationship just felt right. Two old friends who didn't need the hassle of a deeper relationship, that's what they were, and that was fine with Annie.

A crack of thunder startled them all. Annie had almost forgotten that a storm raged outside. For a moment, she'd felt so content and cozy there in the kitchen. Annie shifted in her chair. "I hope Devon's not out in the barn," she said, rising to peer out the window.

"Oh, no, he's upstairs," Bessie reassured her. "I gave him the first cookies out of the oven and I'm sure he shared them with that dog," she laughed. "You know, the puppy and the cat seem to get along just fine," she said. "I'm surprised. I guess the dog's smart enough to keep on TigerLily's good side," she mused.

Annie started to sit back down in her chair when lightning lit up the sky, followed by yet another boom of thunder. The storm was directly overhead now, and Annie could feel a small rumble in her bones as the sound faded. The lights flickered, then went out.

"Oops," Bessie said, swallowing her last mouthful of coffee. "Guess the storm knocked the power out."

Annie sighed. "I'd better go check on the guests. I'm sure the power will be back on in a few minutes, but I don't want them to worry about it." She headed for the sitting room, which was shrouded in darkness. The windows let in a little light, but the sky was so gray that it was insubstantial at best.

"Is everyone alright in here?" she called out.

"Annie? What happened?" Doris's voice called back to her.

Annie let her eyes adjust to the very dim light. She could see that everyone was still where she'd left them. "The storm knocked the power out," she explained. "It should be back on soon. It normally only takes a few minutes for the power company to fix it," she added, hoping to reassure her guests.

"Well, now, isn't this cozy?" Marie's voice called out. "Should we light some candles?"

Annie hesitated. She didn't particularly *want* open flames sitting around the place, not after the fire on the deck, but they *did* need light. "I'll go and get some from the kitchen," she replied. "You all sit tight and I'll be right back."

Annie met Rory in the parlour. "I've got some flashlights out in my truck," he offered. "You want me to run out there and bring them in?" Annie hated to ask him to go out in the rain, but she knew that the power could be out for a while. Although she'd reassured her guests that it would be on soon, she knew from experience that outages this far out in the countryside could last much longer than just a few minutes.

"Okay," she agreed, "but be careful. I don't want you to get struck by lightning," she said earnestly.

Rory left through the front door, and Bessie came from the kitchen. "Is Rory going to get flashlights?" she asked. Annie nodded in the dark hallway. "Good, then I'm going to run upstairs and check on Devon."

"I was just going to grab some candles from the cellar," Annie replied. "Please be careful going up those stairs. It's dark up on the landing and I'd hate it if you fell."

Bessie waved her hand dismissively and started up the stairs. Annie knew she could warn her mother to be careful all day long, but the woman would do as she wanted regardless.

Annie crept through the dark parlour and into the now empty kitchen. The slow cookers still bubbled on the counter. *At least they'll stay warm for a while,* she thought. There was just enough light coming in through the window to illuminate the door to the cellar. Annie pulled it open and instinctively flipped the light switch, then cursed at herself when the light didn't come on.

"Duh, Annie, there's no electricity," she said aloud, bracing herself for the descent into the inky blackness of the windowless cellar. She pulled out her cell phone and used its light to make her way down the stairs for the second time that day. Behind her, the door let in a little light, but it didn't penetrate any further than a few feet.

She reached the bottom of the stairs and shone her light on the shelves, looking for the plastic container that held the candles. There was no label for 'candles,' so she pulled the one out that was labeled 'emergency supplies.' She laughed as she discovered that her mother had placed several packs of miniature candy bars in that container, and she pushed them aside to reveal a box of tea light candles. She pulled them out and left the plastic container where it sat, not willing to try and maneuver the thing back into place on the shelf in the pitch black dark. She was just about to turn around when she heard the door to the cellar slam shut.

Annie's heart jumped into her throat. She took a few deep breaths and tried to calm herself while all sorts of dark thoughts filled her head. Did someone just slam the door closed? Had they known she was in the cellar? Why on earth would someone close a door without calling into the room first?

Forcing herself to calm down, she assessed the situation. *Yes*, the door had slammed, and *yes*, it had frightened her, but it was probably just the wind, or maybe Rory had found the door opened and closed it without realizing she was in the cellar.

Calming her pounding heart, Annie climbed the stairs carefully, clutching the candles to her chest and shining her phone's light on each step as she went. It felt like forever before she reached the top, but she did reach it, with trembling legs and a still-racing pulse. With great relief, she passed her phone to the hand holding the candles and reached for the doorknob.

It wouldn't budge.

She wiggled it and twisted it, but the door was locked, and Annie wasn't going anywhere.

17

Tears, Fears, and Chocolate Bars

Annie told herself not to panic, and she really tried, but her first instinct was not to sit and wait calmly for someone to help her. She banged as hard as she could on the door. It was a solid, sturdy door, and the thick wood muffled the sounds of her hand hitting it. She heard a scuttling, scraping noise and nearly fell down the stairs, trying to see what unimaginable horror could be sneaking its way towards her in the dark.

Her phone cast its glow on the steps below her, and she saw the tealight candles. Her pulse slowed ever so slightly. *Jeez, woman, get a grip*, she mumbled to herself. She bent to retrieve the candles and nearly dropped her phone. Finally, candles in hand and her phone gripped more tightly, she sat down on the top step.

The stress of the day and the horror of being stuck in a dark, dank cellar piled on top of her, and Annie found herself wiping tears from the corners of her eyes. Her phone went dark, so she pressed the button and watched it spring to life once again. At least she had her phone. She glanced at the power level--a measly nineteen percent battery life remained. She hoped that someone would realize she was missing before the battery died, and her tired, tearful brain envisioned her mother finding her skeletal remains sometime in the autumn when she came down to the cellar to look for her hidden chocolate bars.

The screen on her phone went dark once more, and Annie nearly smacked her own forehead. She had a phone. She'd just call someone to open the door, then she would throw the candles at Marie and go up to her room and her soft, comforting bed. Annie flicked the contacts file open and called Rory, but nothing happened. She checked the phone again and found that there were no bars showing at the top--there was no service signal down in the cellar.

Annie let out a long, slow breath. She sat the candles down beside her on the steps, put the phone in her pocket, where it sat snugly, safe from the risk of being dropped onto the hard concrete floor, and she turned to the door once again. She slapped it with her palms and called out, but her own voice just bounced back at her. She balled her hands up into fists and pounded on the wood, but she couldn't make the sound any louder that way. *What the heck was the door made of?* Finally, she gave into her frustration and let out a long, loud, exasperated scream.

Nothing happened.

Annie turned her back to the door and peered down into the velvety blackness. She let her hand drop to the candles, reassuring herself that they were still there. She had the sudden thought that maybe she'd seen matches in the box with the candles, and for a minute she felt a little better. She pulled out her phone, pressed the button to illuminate the screen, and scrambled down the stairs and across the room. The light went out, and she pushed the button again, afraid to fire up the phone properly in case she ran her battery out.

The plastic tub was still sitting where she'd left it, which was on a folding table her mother had assured her would be a fine crafting table for them. She laughed at the thought--she certainly had no time for crafting or hobbies these days. No, Annie Richards was far too busy for scrapbooking or knitting; she was busy finding dead bodies and getting herself locked in creepy old cellars.

Annie shone her phone into the box and picked through its contents. Besides the chocolate bars, there were three boxes of Band-Aids, two tubes of Neosporin, a roll of gauze bandage, a six-pack of bottled water, and a pack of sugarless chewing gum, but definitely no matches.

Annie slapped her hand against the surface of the folding table in frustration. The whole thing wobbled, but it didn't fall over. Feeling foolish, fed up, and frustrated, Annie grabbed a bag of chocolate bars and headed back up the stairs. *If this isn't an emergency,* she thought, *I don't know what is.*

Sitting alone in the dark, Annie opened the bag and unwrapped a chocolate bar, then chewed it thoughtfully. *When I get out of here*, she mused, *I will definitely put some battery-powered lights up in this room.* She ate a couple of the chocolates in silence, then reached up and banged the door a few more times, just in case someone was in the kitchen.

She did this a few more times, then she simply sat in silence. Occasionally she could hear a creak or clicking sound, the sounds that old houses make when you're paying close enough attention to notice them. She let her mind drift, and found herself thinking of a time when she was a girl and had found herself accidentally locked in the bathroom. She must have been five or six years old, very young, and the doorknob in her childhood home had a terrible habit of sticking in the frame.

Annie recalled thinking that she'd have to live in the bathroom, that no one would ever find her and she'd be forced to sleep on the rug in front of the bath tub. She chuckled to herself as she recalled thinking that she could live on toothpaste and water for a few days because she'd seen a documentary on television that told her food was less important than water. Of course, in her panicked state, it hadn't dawned on her that her parents would come looking for her, or, as it just so happened, that her mother would have to use the bathroom only ten minutes after Annie had resigned herself to her doom.

"At least I have water and chocolate," she said aloud into the darkness, though she really wished that she had a toilet, too. She suddenly wished that she hadn't thought about that memory. The diet coke she'd had earlier had been refreshing, but now she was starting to realize that she'd need to go to the bathroom soon, or she'd be in a heap of trouble. She crossed her legs, and tried to distract herself, but it was no good. Now she was stuck in the dark, in a cellar, where no one could hear her, and she had to pee.

Annie almost laughed out loud at her predicament, but she didn't want to risk laughing too hard and having an accident. She was glad that she'd never stopped practicing her kegels because the more she tried not to think about having to go, the more she really needed to. Finally, she couldn't take it anymore.

Rising to her feet, Annie turned and banged on the door once again, but this time, she yelled, too. "Somebody! Mama! Rory! Let me out of this godforsaken cellar! I need to go peeeee!"

At some point during her screaming rant, Annie missed the sound of the lock clicking, and as her fists rained down on the door for the umpteenth time, she suddenly realized that it was moving. Annie fell through the rapidly opening door and into Rory's chest, knocking him to the ground.

"Annie, are you alr--" Rory didn't get the sentence out before she'd knocked the wind out of him, and by the time he'd sat up, she was scrambling out the door, making a beeline for the bathroom.

"Sorry, Rory! Be right back!" she called breathlessly over her shoulder, deftly maneuvering through the house despite the fact that the lights were still out. A few minutes later, she emerged, calmer, less breathless, and still carrying the small pack of candles.

Now that she was in control of her emotions, Annie explained her frantic exit from the cellar. Rory listened, nodding in the dim light and trying not to laugh. Annie was sure her cheeks were glowing in the darkened kitchen. "So, I had to go. Really, really bad. That's why I was screaming."

Rory shook his head. "I'm not sure how you managed to get yourself locked down there in the first place. That's a heavy oak door, so it probably didn't blow shut on its own." He'd answered two of her questions with his statement, but it only raised another one.

"Then how did it slam shut?" She shuddered at the memory. Annie had never thought that she was afraid of the dark, but after being locked in a pitch black cellar, she was starting to think maybe she had a very reasonable fear of dark places.

Rory frowned. "I don't know. I came back in through the kitchen door and walked right past the cellar. It was already closed then. I swear if I'd have heard you banging on the door I would have run to let you out." He seemed to feel so guilty about it all, and Annie realized that he blamed himself for not getting to her sooner.

"I wasn't banging on the door the whole time," she told him, "and I don't think I was making that much noise through that heavy oak," she said, trying to make him feel better. "But someone had to have shut the door."

"You think it was your Mama? Maybe she didn't realize you were down there."

Annie thought this over for half a second. "No, she would have yelled down, I'm sure of it. Someone slammed that door. It wasn't closed gently." She shook the box of tea lights. "I don't suppose you have any matches?"

Rory suppressed a laugh. Annie suppressed the desire to hit him. "What? What are you laughing at?"

Rory walked over to the refrigerator and reached up on top. He pulled down a metal cookie tin and sat it on the counter by the window. In the dim light, Annie could just make out a box of tealight candles just like the one she had in her hand and a box of matches.

"I made your mama keep these in the kitchen in case of emergencies," he explained. "I didn't want her stumbling down those cellar steps in the dark."

Annie's mouth fell open and she snapped it shut. "Well, then--" She was angry and annoyed, and momentarily speechless. She snatched the matches from the box with a mumbled 'thank you', then headed for the sitting room.

It was empty.

"You've got to be kidding me!" Annie pulled a single candle out and lit it, then sat it on the mantel of the fireplace. Its meager light wasn't as reassuring as she'd hoped, so she lit another one and placed it a few inches away. "Where is everyone?" she asked.

Rory stood in the doorway. "I have no idea. Everybody was gone when I got back." He motioned towards the coffee table. "I left a couple of flashlights there for the guests to use. There are a couple more in the kitchen." He clicked his own on, and a blinding beam of light appeared. "You be Scully, I'll be Mulder," he teased, handing her a flashlight. "Let's see if they've all been abducted by aliens."

Annie grinned and clicked on her own flashlight. "I guess we should check upstairs, make sure Mama and Devon are okay." Annie imagined her mother falling in the dimly lit hallway upstairs, or tripping over something in the dark. At Bessie's age, a fall could be downright deadly. Annie tried not to let those thoughts take hold, and she forced herself to think of something else.

A quick look upstairs found Devon and the dog stretched out on Devon's bed. TigerLily sat on the windowsill of the large picture window in the middle of the room, her feline outline highlighted by the occasional flash of lightning.

"Did your grandmother come in here?" Annie asked, pulling Devon's attention from the video he was watching on his phone.

"Yep,"

"And she left again?"

"Yep." Devon let out an exaggerated sigh. "Jeez, Mom, don't tell me you lost Granny Bessie. I guess it's a miracle you've managed to keep track of me all these years."

Annie shook her head at his sarcasm. "Just stay up here until the power comes on, will you?"

Devon waved his hand in a 'whatever' gesture. Annie stepped back out of the room and pulled the door closed.

"He's got his own little menagerie in there, doesn't he?" Rory joked.

"Oh, yeah," she replied. "This place is turning into a real zoo."

They went back downstairs and headed towards the back of the house, checking empty rooms as they went. Finally, they stepped onto the screened in back porch and were greeted by Bessie's cheerful voice.

"Oh, there you are! I was starting to get worried about you

two," she teased. "But, as long as you were together, that's alright then."

Annie ignored her mother's not-so-subtle hint about wanting them to be a couple again and bluntly addressed the group.

"What are y'all doing out here? You do realize that there's a thunderstorm going on out here?" She looked around. Rob and Kizzy had rejoined the group, looking much better than they had earlier that day.

"It was Marie's idea," Kizzy replied. "She suggested we watch the storm. It sure is pretty," she added. "Like a little light show."

Bessie waved her hand dismissively. "Oh, they're alright out here. It's not like we're running around out in the storm. Besides, it's passing now. Don't you remember how you and your daddy would sit out under the carport and watch the storms when you were little?"

Annie did remember that, but she said nothing about it. Instead, she pulled her mother aside. "Somebody shut the cellar door and locked it while I was still in the cellar. Do you know anything about that?"

Bessie's eyes grew wide. "Oh, my goodness! No, I don't know who would do such a thing! Oh, I bet it was dark in there--"

Annie cut her off. She didn't want to relive her adventure in the cellar. "It's alright, Rory let me out. But I want to know who could have locked me in there and why." She looked around at the motley group of guests. "Did anybody follow me to the kitchen?"

Bessie thought for a moment. "I don't think so. Just after you left, Frank went upstairs to get his blood pressure medicine," she offered, "but he came right back. And Marie came out here--that's how come we're all out here now. She came back and told us to come watch the lightning, and we've been out here ever since."

Annie frowned. "When did Kizzy and Rob come down?" She

hadn't heard anyone coming or going from behind the thick oak cellar door.

"Oh, they came down with Frank. I asked Devon if he wanted to come down with us, but he was watching theYuletubes on his phone," she added, cheerfully oblivious that she'd said gotten the name wrong.

Annie gritted her teeth. Frank had been alone when she'd been locked in the cellar. And so had Kizzy and Marie. Any of them could have locked her in--accidentally or on purpose--and she had no idea who it was without asking them directly. The idea of asking her guests if they'd locked her in the cellar didn't exactly appeal to Annie, but it really needed to be done. After all, what if it had been her mother locked inside the dark room or Devon?

Thinking it best to just ask everyone at once, Annie cleared her throat. She was just trying to find the best way to broach the subject when the lights on the veranda flickered to life.

A chorus of cheers went up, and a few sighs of relief, too. Annie didn't get a chance to ask anyone about the cellar door because her guests were already filing into the house, following Bessie, whose Pied Piper promises of dinner were too good to pass up. Annie and Rory stayed behind on the veranda for a moment.

"You okay?" he asked her. Somehow, despite their having been apart for nearly two decades, Rory always seemed to know when something was bothering her.

Annie shrugged. "Well, I think that somebody dislikes me enough to lock my in my own cellar, but I can't tell who that is. And someone set fire to my deck, but nobody has a clue who it was. Oh, and let's not forget the fact that two of my guests were poisoned by who-knows-what while on a fishing trip that I suggested. Maybe Marie's right. Maybe there's a vengeful spirit hanging around here, making my life miserable, just for kicks."

She said this last sentence with plenty of sarcasm, just in case Rory thought she was serious about the ghost part.

Rory looked at her for a long moment. "Well, I think you work too hard and you're worn out from running around here taking care of everybody. Why don't we go get some supper and eat out on the front porch? I'll show you my sketches for the Man-cave," he joked.

"I'm sure your handyman quarters will be the smartest in the state," she quipped. A tired smile found its way onto her lips. "The front porch sounds like the perfect place for dinner. I'm sure Mama can keep the guests entertained for one evening. After all, it's not like anything else can go wrong today."

Annie felt a cool breeze drift in through the screens on the back porch. It sent a slight chill down her spine, and although she didn't know it at the time, she'd come to regret that last statement sooner than she'd realize.

18

Discussing Death at the Dinner Table

Dinner was later than Bessie had planned, thanks to the storm and the resulting power outage. By the time she'd sat the piping hot cornbread on the table, everyone was ravenous. Despite the long day, Bessie was in fine form at the dinner table, regaling her guests with stories about her childhood, the town's history, and even a few local legends, including the story that most believed about Rosewood Place (but that wasn't really true).

"Oh, people have called this place cursed for years," she admitted openly, "but that's mostly because it failed as a plantation. The crops didn't do so well," she explained, "and nobody ever seemed to hang around long enough to do anything with the place. Some say that there's a hidden treasure on this very property that dates back to the pre-civil war era," she teased.

"Well, is there?" Mr. George had paused mid-bite, his spaghetti hung precariously on his fork as he waited for her reply.

Bessie smiled innocently. "Well, let me just put it this way. I've never seen a treasure here, but it's a lovely thought, just the same." She took a sip of her tea. She'd put more sugar in it than usual tonight and brewed it just a little stronger than she normally would. It was what her daughter would undoubtedly refer to as 'rocket fuel' since the sugary, caffeinated drink would give anyone a boost of energy after drinking it.

Mr. George seemed to ponder this as he chewed. Bessie liked the man, despite his odd personality. She had begun to think of him as some sort of quiet genius after he'd quoted page after page of statistics about old homes. She'd heard him tell Rob that he read a great deal of books about historical homes and other buildings, and he happened to have a near photographic memory. Bessie wished her memory was half as good. At nearly seventy, she was still sharp as a tack, but a photographic memory would be an amazingly useful thing to have, she reckoned.

Kizzy Fitzsimmons and Rob Reynolds seemed awfully cozy, she noted. In Bessie's mind, it would be a grand thing if the two youngsters fell in love during their stay at Rosewood Place. She allowed herself a few minutes to daydream about renting them the barn for their wedding--once it had been renovated, of course--and she wondered whether she'd be able to find someone to come in and cater such an event.

Frank and Doris had been discussing taking a drive into town the next day. Doris wanted to take a look at a couple of houses that they'd seen advertised online, Frank wanted to investigate the town's barbecue restaurant. Bessie hoped that the couple would decide to settle in or around Coopersville. They were a terribly nice pair of people, despite Frank's occasional gruff attitude.

Devon had graced the group with his presence for all of five minutes, long enough to help himself to a second portion of spaghetti. She marveled at the skinny teen's ability to put away food; he ate like a horse but never seemed to gain a single ounce. If anything, she worried that he might be losing weight. Of course, he'd grown two inches since he'd moved back to South

Carolina, proof, in her mind, that sunshine and fresh air could make almost anything thrive.

Bessie wiped the corner of her mouth and let her eyes drift down the table to Marie Robichaud. Marie was the one guest that Bessie hadn't really spoken to at length. Yes, the woman always seemed to be there, wherever Bessie went, but for all of Marie's intrusive appearances, the woman said very little to those around her, apart from making the occasional comment about spirits and ghosts and whatnot.

Bessie believed in the supernatural. She believed in ghosts, especially now since she'd moved into Rosewood Place. Of course, she'd never seen a ghost at the old plantation house, but she could imagine the spirits of long dead residents wandering around late at night when it was silent and peaceful. However, Bessie didn't buy Marie's story about angry spirits hanging around the place. Despite the fact that there had been three murders right on this very farm, and quite possibly more that had happened in the preceding centuries, Bessie had never once felt afraid of an evil spirit.

Now, evil living people, that was another matter entirely.

Bessie may not have feared evil spirits, but she knew enough to be wary of those living souls who'd just as soon put you in the ground as look at you. Bessie liked to think of herself as a good judge of character, and she'd certainly had it right when she had correctly suspected Suzy Anderson's killer back in the spring. Bessie had learned to trust her instincts when it came to people, and it had never served her wrong so far in life.

Bessie loved a good murder mystery novel as much as the next gal, but she never in a million years envisioned that she'd be caught up in not one, but two murders, all right under her very own roof. Or, in the case of Mr. Lou Ross, in her backyard pond.

"Have you learned anything else about Mr. Ross?" Marie's question startled Bessie somewhat. Marie seemed to ask about the very thing that Bessie was thinking of, despite the fact that she'd said nothing about the dead man all day.

"Oh, well," she began, "I probably shouldn't say, you know, because of the ongoing investigation."

Marie smiled. "Has Mr. Barnes spoken to any more of the guests?" She looked thoughtful for a moment. "Emmett, that's his name, isn't it?"

Bessie felt her cheeks flush just the tiniest bit. That always happened when someone asked her about Emmett, even if they were just asking about his name. "Yes, Emmett Barnes. He's been our Police Chief for years. He's a good man and an excellent policeman. If anyone can get to the bottom of this sad, sad situation, it's Emmett and his officers."

Marie's smile drifted away. She leaned towards Bessie, which wasn't easy since she was on the opposite side of the table. "Can I tell you something?" She asked in a way that made Bessie feel only slightly uncomfortable. Bessie got the distinct impression that Marie wanted to tell her something in confidence, but sitting at the busy dining room table, it hardly made sense to tell it here.

Marie didn't wait for a response. "I get the distinct feeling that Mr. Ross is still with us, spiritually, I mean. I feel as though his spirit can't leave--as though he has unfinished business in this world." She put her hand over her eyes. "I don't normally get such a strong reading," she confessed, "but here, in this lovely old house, the spirits are very loud."

Bessie didn't dismiss Marie's statement, but she didn't encourage her to say more. Instead, she smiled and nodded her head. "What is it you do again, dear?"

Marie removed her hand from her eyes. "I do many things. I

152

have a very strong link to the spirit world, you see, and I often send and receive messages for people."

"Like the Long Island Medium on television?" Bessie had become fascinated by the woman on that television program after her dear husband, Robert Purdy, had passed away some years before.

"Oh, well, yes, I suppose I do some of the same things," Marie replied, "but I also do spiritual advising, you know, tarot readings, aura assessments, that sort of thing. You'd be surprised how many people simply neglect to consider their spiritual well-being," she confided. "I've been communicating with the dead since I was girl, you know. I woke up one day and my grandmother was sitting on the end of my bed, smiling at me, which was very confusing because she'd died the week before."

Bessie nearly choked on the tea she was drinking. "Oh, my! Were you frightened?"

"Of course not! She only wanted to wish me well and tell me that we would meet again, and we did. She visits me often, you know."

"Oh," Bessie replied. "I hope she knows that there's a surcharge for extra guests in a room," she joked. Marie didn't laugh. "That must be a terribly fascinating career," she added, hoping she hadn't offended the woman.

"It can be. I have helped many people," she stated simply. "That's probably why this Lou Ross fellow is bothering me so. I fear he expects me to help him with his unfinished business, whatever that may be, but I have nothing to go on, no idea of where to start."

The idea of a dead man having unfinished business was both ridiculous and a little sad to Bessie. On one hand, he was dead. Nothing that anyone did could change that, so anything the man had left to do on this earth couldn't be that important, especially if it involved being a con artist.

On the other hand, a repentant ghost who wanted to make things right, well, that sounded like quite a nice idea. Bessie wondered for a moment if ghost Lou had undergone a change of heart--perhaps he wanted to confess his crimes from beyond the grave or even help give his victims back the money that he'd stolen from them. Bessie's curiosity began to stir, which was never a good thing.

"It's the strangest thing," Bessie confided, "but I remember Annie telling me that he had a mother in Mobile--Alabama, I presume--but he didn't list her as a next of kin. You know, we always try to put someone down in case, heaven forbid, something bad happens."

Marie nodded. "Makes perfect sense. Did he mention her name, perhaps? I'm sure if we knew who she was we could try to find out where she lives, maybe pass on a message for Mr. Ross."

Bessie shook her head. "No name. Annie spoke with Emmett about it, though, so maybe the police can track the woman down and notify her of his passing." She suddenly remembered what Annie had told her about the man having a package delivered to the house. "Oh, and it's so sad, but Mr. Ross was planning to have a package delivered right here to the house. He'd told Annie that he was having a gift for his mother delivered to him while he stayed with us. I guess she'll never get it now," she added, shaking her head.

Marie's eyes grew large. "Has Annie received the package yet? That may be why his spirit is so restless--he wants the package to reach the rightful owner."

Bessie hesitated. "Well, she received a couple of packages this morning, but I have no idea if either of them belonged to Mr.

Ross. She was so busy with the power outage, I believe she just stuck them in the office and forgot all about them. I suppose I'd better remind her to be on the lookout for his package in particular. She'll want to take it to Emmett as soon as she gets it, though. After all, if anyone can figure out who and where Mr. Ross's mother is, Emmett and the police can."

Marie narrowed her eyes. "I didn't want to say anything because I know that Annie gets upset when I mention my *talents*, but I'm not sure that the fire was an accident. Neither was Rob and Kizzy's illness. You know, they were the last ones on the deck the night that poor Mr. Ross died."

Bessie leaned forward, trying to close the gap between Marie and herself. She glanced at the other guests, who were at the far end of the table and likely out of earshot, but she didn't want them to think she was talking about any of them. "What do you mean? Did you see something?"

Marie cast her eyes down the table towards the other guests. "I don't want to say anything here," she said quietly. "Why don't we finish our chat in the sitting room?"

Bessie felt guilty for talking about the other guests behind their backs. "I'd really ought to be getting these dishes cleared away," she apologized. "And I'm not as young as I used to be. I'm absolutely worn out from today. Maybe we can sit and have a chat tomorrow over a nice cup of tea. I'd bet you're an Earl Grey fan, am I right?" Bessie shifted the conversation as she stood.

Marie took the hint. "That would be lovely," she replied. "Would you like some help with these?" She gestured towards the dishes.

"Oh, no, that's alright. Annie will be in here in a minute to help. You just let your food settle and enjoy the evening." Bessie picked up several plates and balanced them carefully, then backed out of the dining room. As she walked towards the kitchen, she had the awful feeling that perhaps she'd said too much to Marie. After all, Lou's death was still an ongoing investigation, and Annie had told her to be careful about what she said around the guests. Still, she supposed that if Marie was the real deal, she'd already know most of what the police did anyway.

Bessie decided that she'd make sure that the next time she spoke to Marie, she'd let the psychic do most of the talking. As she loaded dirty dishes into the dishwasher, Bessie decided that she'd also better not say anything to her daughter about her chat with Marie. At best, Annie would laugh at her for even entertaining the idea that Marie could actually communicate with the dead. At worst, Bessie would be in big trouble for spilling the beans about the mysterious package that was supposed to be delivered for the dead man.

Still, something else worried at Bessie's heart. What if Marie really could communicate with the dead? Could a simple ritual like a seance solve a murder? Shouldn't they at least try if it meant that a killer could be brought to justice? Bessie also had another thought, one that she didn't quite want to linger on. If Marie could speak to those who'd passed, did that mean that she could contact Robert, too? She pushed that thought away as quickly as it formed and brought her focus back to the dirty dishes in front of her.

With a surprising burst of energy (probably from the super-sweet iced tea,) Bessie finished clearing the dinner dishes on her own, then slipped up to her bedroom for some peace, quiet, and to enjoy her current murder mystery novel, though these days, real life was beginning to become far more interesting than the mysteries on the pages of her books.

19

Birdwatching and Boxes

Midweek in Coopersville was hardly what Annie Richards would call a 'bustling time.' After living in New York City for the better part of two decades, it was impossible to compare the two towns. After all, Coopersville only boasted a population of just under two thousand people, most of which, like Annie, lived on the outer edges of the town, all spread out and nicely separated by lots of grass, trees, and wild spaces.

In the heart of town itself, there was a vibrant little community built up around small businesses and the parts of a town that kept it functioning: the post office, the police station, and a little further out, the elementary, middle, and high schools. Boutiques and specialty shops lined Main Street, branching out in spidery waves down quaint streets with names like Macadamia Avenue and Chockaree Road. The heart of the city had received a fairly recent renovation that saw a beautification of the old town. The police station had benefitted from this with the introduction of pedestrian benches and pretty floral landscaping.

Annie's own realtor had a business just off of Main Street. Debbie Schipper had been helping pair home buyers and sellers for the better part of three decades. She seldom traveled further than the neighboring cities surrounding Coopersville, but she had all the work she could handle. The past ten years had seen a steady influx of northerners and retirees who dreamed of mild southern winters and friendly, smiling faces in their golden years. An influx of big businesses in some of the neighboring cities also meant a boom for Coopersville real estate, as many folks preferred the small town life to accompany their 'big city' jobs.

Annie had been happy to send Frank and Doris to see Debbie. She owed her realtor a huge debt of gratitude for helping Annie find and buy Rosewood Place so quickly. Debbie seemed to know the right people to make things happen in the real estate world, and Annie hoped that would mean that she'd make good things happen for the Martins, too, although she was well aware that, being from Up North, Debbie wouldn't be quite as motivated to rush their buying process.

It was a well-known, little-discussed fact that although folks born and raised south of the Mason-Dixon line were as polite as punch to everyone they met, they prioritized their own when it came to filling up houses in genteel southern towns and communities. Annie knew that Debbie's own daughter had married a boy from Indiana, so Frank and Doris at least had a sympathetic realtor in Mrs. Schipper.

While the Martins perused houses and barbecue menus, Rob and Kizzy spent the morning playing cards in the sitting room. Bessie, feeling guilty about leaving dinner until so late the day before, made sure that breakfast was over-the-top, a southern fried feast of eggs, bacon, sausage, biscuits, gravy, grits, and country ham that would have given Cracker Barrel a run for its money. The young news anchor and the unemployed actress stuffed themselves silly on her home cooked goodness, then agreed that it was too hot to venture outdoors, but a deck of playing cards and plenty of good conversation was always a great way to waste a morning.

Alexander George returned to his room after breakfast. Before he went back upstairs he made a detour to the little library off the sitting room. Judging by the stack of books he carried, Annie reckoned they might not see him again until dinner time.

Annie would have loved to have spent the morning sipping coffee out by the pond, reading a trashy romance novel or even working through a sudoku puzzle, but the realities of running a bed-and-breakfast were staring her in the face, so she grabbed her cleaning supplies and her master set of keys and began making a pass through each guest's room, running the vacuum cleaner quickly over rugs, sweeping a light scattering of dust bunnies and dried grass tracked in from outside, and gathering laundry from the guest rooms as well as her own family's quarters.

For the most part, Annie liked to make the guests feel as if they were simply hanging out in their own homes, so she did allow them to do their own laundry if they wanted. So far, she'd only had to wash mostly towels, a few shirts, and just a handful of unmentionables, which were thankfully fairly harmless. After having been married for many years and a mother to a teenaged son, Annie knew the worst laundry horrors were likely yet to come, though she hoped that guests with hygiene problems opted to do their own laundry.

She spent a couple of hours upstairs, interrupted by quick visits to the laundry room and kitchen (some guests had a terrible habit of taking midnight snacks to bed and not returning the dishes to the kitchen). It crossed her mind that she wouldn't always be so lucky with her timing. Most of the guest rooms were empty, which made cleaning much easier, but she couldn't get into Mr. George's room or Marie's. The self-proclaimed psychic had requested that her room be left unattended, which was fine by Annie. She supposed that it only meant more work when the woman left, but Annie had no desire to upset her guest and no reason to suspect that Marie was making any sort of huge messes in the room.

After finishing the upstairs cleaning, Annie grabbed a can of diet soft drink from the fridge and headed out to the back porch for a break. She hoped that Rory wasn't busy working on his latest project or finishing off repairs to the deck. She thought it might be nice to sit and chat with him about--she realized with a start that she didn't really have anything in mind to discuss with him, she just felt like hanging out and feeling some normalcy again. It had been such an odd, stressful week, despite the joy of seeing her hard work come to life in the bed-and-breakfast.

The spring-loaded screen door slammed shut behind her before Annie realized that she wasn't alone on the screened-in porch. "Mama, Miss Robichaud, I didn't know y'all were out here." Annie cringed at how easily she'd slipped back into her southern drawl after only a few months back in the south. "Birdwatching?" she asked, noting a small pair of binoculars and a book about wildlife lying on a table between the two seated women.

"Oh, Annie! Come here and look at this bird," Bessie greeted her. "I swear I just saw one of these sitting right on the edge of the deck down there."

Annie glanced at the deck. It looked as good as new thanks to Rory. He was nowhere to be seen, so she assumed he must be with Devon out in the barn, playing with the dog or working on his designs for the new groundskeeper's lodge.

"Which bird is that?" Annie asked, following her mother's pointing finger to a picture of a pretty little green and yellow bird with a blue face.

"It's called a Mourning Warbler," Bessie replied proudly. "I don't think these are too common around these parts, at least not during the summer. The book says they migrate south in the fall," she added with an expert nod.

Marie sniffed. "It's here because it's in mourning, I'm sure." She smiled at Annie, then glanced at Bessie. "Should we ask her now, Bessie?"

Annie looked at her mother, who looked just a little bit guilty of something. "Annie, dear, I've been thinking." Bessie thinking too hard about anything wasn't a good sign, but Annie didn't interrupt her to say so. "All these strange things we've had going on around here--the fire, the guests getting sick--don't you think it's odd?"

Annie wiped condensation from her unopened can of drink against her shirt, leaving a dark streak of moisture. "Well, yeah, I'd say it's pretty odd," she replied sarcastically.

"I've been discussing it with Marie, and the more that I think about things, the more I think that it couldn't hurt to use her, well, her *services*," she said, emphasizing the last word.

Annie could feel the heat seeping through the screens from outside. How on earth was her mother not dying out here in this heat? "What on earth are you talking about?" Her response came out crabbier than she'd meant it to. Annie made a mental note to be more careful when responding to questions or comments about her guests' careers in the future.

"Well, why don't we let Marie try to talk to Mr. Ross and see what it is he wants from all of us?" Bessie took a sip of her peppermint tea and licked her lips. "After all, it's what she does for a living," she added.

Annie pulled a chair over to the little table where the other two women were sitting. It wasn't meant to seat three people, and she hardly had room to sit her Diet Coke, but she plonked it down anyway. "Well, Mother, I'm not sure that would work. You know, because he's dead and all."

Marie inclined her head slightly. Her frizzy hair moved in the warm breeze that blew across the porch. "I can still communicate with him, Annie. I just need something that belonged to him so I can call him over from wherever he's hovering," she replied simply, as though she'd just explained how to bake a cake or change a lightbulb instead of how to talk to a dead man.

"I'm sorry, Marie, but I'm just not sure about that. I don't know how I feel about that sort of thing," Annie replied, struggling to find a way to say no that wouldn't offend the psychic. She was proud of herself for at least not laughing at the suggestion, but she couldn't find a way of telling Marie that she didn't believe in communicating with spirits without cracking up in laughter.

Bessie put her hand on Annie's arm. Her skin was soft and cool against Annie's own. "Let's not say no just yet. I've been thinking about it for a while now, and it couldn't hurt anything, could it?"

"Yes, it could," Annie replied. "It could freak out our guests and give us the kind of reputation that we really don't want to have," she said firmly.

"We don't have to involve the others," Marie piped up. "In fact, the fewer people we have, the better. We could limit this to just the three of us, that's enough people to provide the spiritual energy that I need to complete the ritual."

"Ritual?" Annie's eyebrows went up.

"Seance, communication ritual--call it what you like. I just need something that belonged to the dead man and I can ask him why he won't leave you alone."

"Why do you think these strange happenings have anything to

do with ghosts?" Annie asked. "Ghosts don't usually need to use lighter fluid to start fires," she challenged.

"Ghosts, as you call them, use whatever they can to get your attention. Don't you think it's odd that the only part of the deck that was burned was the part near where the body was discovered?" Marie asked. "And what about the fact that only Kizzy and Rob have been sick? They were the last ones on the deck the night that Mr. Ross died," she added.

Annie was in no way convinced that either of those two incidents were in the least bit supernatural, but she was curious about why on earth Marie had her heart set on speaking with the ghost of the dead man.

"Your mother told me that you were locked in the cellar the day of the storm." Marie's words pulled Annie to attention. "Don't you wonder how on earth that could have happened when everyone else in the house was together in another room?" she asked, arching one eyebrow. "Something in this house is trying to communicate with us, Annie. We'd be foolish not to listen."

The hairs on the back of Annie's neck gave an involuntary shiver. "Even if I agreed that you could do this, I'm afraid that I don't have anything that belonged to the dead man."

"Annie, what about the package?" Bessie's voice was hopeful. "If we had that, we could use it, couldn't we?"

"I don't think so. When that package arrives--if it arrives--we'll have to turn it over to the police. You can't just open packages that don't belong to you, even if you think you can use what's inside to ask the dead person who killed him." Annie popped the top on her can and took a long sip of her drink. She glanced at the binoculars on the table again. "Wait, are those Dad's?"

Bessie blushed slightly. "Yes, you remember when you used to go birdwatching with him? I kept them for Devon. I thought he might like to have something that belonged to his grandfather some day."

"We wouldn't have to open it," Marie interjected before Annie could say anything else. "The package, I mean. I would simply need to hold it during the ceremony. As long as he had some sort of attachment to the item, it should work."

"Didn't you say it was meant to be a gift for his mother?" Bessie asked.

Annie didn't want to discuss the matter anymore, but she didn't want to shoot her mother and Marie's plan down without some small mercy. It bothered her that her mother actually put stock in Marie's words, and it worried her more that she'd bothered to dig out her father's binoculars which, to Annie's knowledge, had been packed away in a box at the back of her mother's closet since they'd moved into Rosewood place six months before. She hoped that Bessie didn't actually believe that Marie could communicate with the dead, and she prayed that the woman hadn't already put some twisted idea of trying to reach Annie's father from beyond the grave into her mother's head, too.

"Let me think about this, okay?" Annie wouldn't commit to an answer, but she wouldn't give an outright 'no' to their idea, either. If Bessie wanted to find some sort of closure in a silly ceremony, maybe letting Marie try talking to Lou Ross--and failing--would let the old woman down gently. "I'll talk to you about it later, okay, Mama?"

Annie waited for Bessie to nod in agreement, then she rose and took her drink from the table. "I think I'll go put this on some ice. Y'all don't sit out here too long in this heat, okay?"

Annie left the two women sitting with their tea and headed back into the house, stopping long enough to fill a glass with crushed ice and the remains of her drink. Her stomach grumbled despite its heavy breakfast, and Annie was surprised to find that it was after noon. She put a straw in her glass and headed for the privacy of her office so she could think over her mother's latest request.

Annie felt something brush past her leg as she pushed the door open. TigerLily. She looked down just in time to see the feline shoot past her and head for the kitchen. "How in the heck do you keep getting in here?" she yelled after the cat, then laughed at herself for bothering to ask. TigerLily was like the anti-Houdini of cats. She could get into all kinds of trouble, but she never seemed to be able to escape it.

Annie stepped into the small office prepared for chaos, but she was pleased that very little seemed to be disturbed, for the most part. The formerly closed up little room greeted her with an earthy fragrance that she didn't expect, and although it didn't exactly stink, it didn't smell like it should. Annie made a mental note to clean the rug that sat beneath her chair just in case TigerLily had used it for a potty while she'd been trapped in the office.

The garbage had been overturned again, but Annie had kept her desk free of loose papers that the kitty was so fond of scattering. As she picked up the empty cup that once held pens and pencils (which were scattered all over the floor of the little room,) Annie noticed a package on the floor.

She suddenly remembered sending Rory in with two packages, but when Annie looked around the office, she could only find one. "Hmm, that's strange," she said aloud. Annie had long ago given up the notion that talking to one's self was anything odd. If it was a sign of madness, she was too far gone into the land of loony to care. She picked up the package and hefted it between her hands, trying to guess what was inside.

It was the smaller of the two packages, if she remembered correctly. She tried to think back to her order, but it had been a couple of weeks since she'd completed it online. Maybe it was the new phone case and required reading book she'd ordered for Devon? It could have been pencils, pens, and index cards, too. She almost shoved the box into a drawer for later, but something odd on the label caught her eye.

The white address label stood out in stark contrast against the dirty brown cardboard box. It looked like the kind of sticky label that you could find in any office supply store, the kind with rounded edges and usually lackluster stickiness. Sure enough, this label was already peeling at the edges, giving it a dirty, cheaper look than she'd expect from one of the big stores that she usually ordered from.

The upper part of the label was jagged, torn in transit, no doubt. Annie could clearly read the words 'In Care Of Annie Richards' right before the address, but there *had been* something else printed just above that. Curiosity got the better of her, and she reached for the scissors in her desk drawer. With a flick and a slice, she cut through the packaging tape that held the box closed. Styrofoam peanuts fell out like little fat snowflakes and drifted onto the floor around her.

Beneath the styrofoam was a filmy layer of tissue paper, and Annie's brain strained to think of what she'd ordered that could have possibly required such protective packaging. She tipped the foam peanuts onto her desk and lifted the tissue paper to reveal a small mahogany-colored box with what looked like a cheap mother-of-pearl inlaid design on the lid. It was about as big as a cigar box and opened much the same way.

"What on earth are you?" she asked the little box as she slipped it out of its packaging. The box glinted under the ceiling lights.

Annie opened it up and admired the pretty green felt inside. *A jewelry box.* She sniffed the wood, wondering if the box had been what she smelled when she'd entered the room, but the box didn't really have any scent to it, apart from the metallic tang of the metal hinges and the nondescript greenness of whatever cheap wood had been used to make it.

A sudden, horrible thought filled Annie's head. Hadn't she been told to expect a package for Mr. Ross? And hadn't he told her himself that it would contain a gift for his mother? Possibly even a jewelry box like the one she now held in her hands, that she'd opened, unwrapped, and *sniffed*, of all things?

"Crap." Annie used the edge of her shirt to wipe her very visible fingerprints from the outside of it, then placed it carefully back into the box, wrapped in the tissue paper. She crammed the foam peanuts back inside, then put the entire box into her deepest desk drawer and locked it.

She'd have to call Emmett. He'd definitely need to know that she'd received the anticipated package, and she'd have to confess to him that she'd opened it, which she was sure was some sort of federal offense. With a groan, Annie placed her head down on her desk and let out a long, frustrated sigh. *Well*, she thought, *I suppose Marie can do her seance now.*

20

Annie Makes a Plan

Rory ran the water in the guest bathroom sink until he was satisfied that he'd cleared the blockage that Annie had asked him to fix. Annie admired him for tackling the plumbing jobs--he was a carpenter, not a plumber--but he wasn't afraid to take on most of the minor plumbing issues they'd had at the old plantation farmhouse, and they'd certainly had more than their share.

"I think that'll do it," he told her. "Just drop a hint to Kizzy that makeup sponges do not belong in drains," he added, tossing a blackened sponge into the trash.

"I'm sure it was an accident," Annie defended her guest. "And you've got it all fixed now, so let's just leave it." She held her hand out to take the empty bucket he was trying to juggle along with a toolbox, plunger, and bottle of vinegar, which they'd used with some baking soda to flush the sink's drain after the blockage was cleared. Rory handed her the bucket but kept everything else. Annie noticed that he had a hard time letting people help him with things, which was silly since he helped practically everyone who asked him for help and sometimes those who didn't.

They carried the things downstairs and out to the barn, which had become Rory's temporary headquarters. He had repaired a few minor leaks in the barn's roof and now the building was the ideal place for him to stash his tools and ongoing repair projects. One such project--a new spindle for the staircase's banister--sat in a lathe in one corner of the barn. Annie loved to peek in and see what Rory was working on at any given time. She rarely told him what to repair or replace, just let him get on with keeping the place looking and functioning beautifully.

"So, I received a package," she said casually, passing the empty bucket to him so he could hang it from a nail on the wall of the barn.

"Another one? What's that, like three in two days? Gotta stop that late night shopping," he teased.

"No, this was one of the ones we picked up the other day. Did you put them both in my office, by the way? I could only find one of them."

Rory nodded. "I sat them both on your desk, the little one on top. Why?"

"Well, I only found one of them, the smaller one," she added. "Anyway, I opened it."

Rory looked at her, waiting for further clarification. "And?"

"I don't think I was supposed to," she said, lowering her voice despite the fact that they were alone. "Rory, I think I opened Lou Ross's package by mistake."

It took Rory a moment to digest what she'd just said. "You what? Annie, you know that opening someone else's mail is a federal offense, right?"

She put her face in her hands. "I didn't know it was his package," she said through her fingers. "The label was torn and my name was written on there, too. You know, 'in care of'?" She pushed her hands through her hair and lifted it off her neck. She wished she'd put it up in a ponytail while she'd been in the house because the heat and humidity outside was making it stick to her.

"Well, that's probably alright, then," he reasoned. "If your name was on the package, you're probably okay." He cocked his head to one side. "So, what was inside?"

She blushed. "It was a jewelry box. He did say he was having something delivered for his mother," she added. "You want to hear something weird?" Rory nodded. "The return address on the package was Lou's home address. At least, it was the home address he gave me when he booked his room."

"So?"

"Well, why would he mail something to himself from himself? I mean, I could understand ordering something online and having it delivered to wherever you were staying, but mailing something to yourself from home? Don't you think that's really odd?"

"Yeah, I do." Rory had been leaning against the wall of the barn, but now he stepped away from it towards Annie. "Why would you mail something to yourself when you could just pack it up in your luggage?"

Annie thought about the state of Lou's car. Emmett had told them that it had been ransacked, torn apart in someone's search for *something*. "Maybe he was worried that someone would find the box. Remember, Emmett told us that someone had been looking for something inside Lou's car the night he died. What if Lou Ross expected someone to be searching for that box, so he hid it by mailing it to himself?"

Rory thought about this for a minute. "Well, he sure didn't expect someone to kill him, did he? I mean, he brought the dog with him. You wouldn't do that if you thought you were going to be murdered." He wiped the sleeve of his shirt, brushing away some dirt. "You know you're going to have to call Emmett and tell him about this."

"Yeah, I know. I almost just want to tape it back up and forget I ever opened it," she admitted. "But I think I have a better plan."

Annie had been thinking about her mother's request to let Marie perform a seance. She hadn't really been entertaining the idea seriously until she'd noticed the return address on the package. Her mind had been working overtime, considering all the reasons why a man might want to send something as unimportant as a cheap jewelry box to himself in the mail. When she'd recalled the state of Lou's car after his body was found, the pieces of the puzzle started falling into place. Someone wanted something that Lou had, and if they'd found it, one of her guests would probably have checked out by now.

"Someone wanted something in Lou's car, right?" She waited for Rory to nod before she continued. "I'm thinking that if they found what they were looking for, they would have just left by now, right? I mean, that is if the person who searched the car is the same person who killed Lou Ross.

"So, if the killer didn't find what they were looking for, maybe they stayed because they either didn't want to look suspicious or maybe they thought they might just find whatever it was they were searching for if they kept looking long enough."

Rory's eyes told Annie that he was mulling this scenario over. "But why stay if they weren't sure that the mystery item would even turn up? I mean, that's a long shot, right?"

"What if they had no plans after leaving here? What if they didn't really know their next move, but just needed a few days to lay low? If they weren't already a suspect, why would they do something as suspicious as to cancel their vacation halfway through?" Annie knew that her suspicions were a long shot, but her gut was telling her that the killer was still at the house.

"So how does the package help us figure out who killed Lou

Ross?"

Annie grinned. "We can use it to lure out whoever killed him," she answered confidently.

Rory crossed his arms. "And how do you plan to do that?"

"We'll let my mother talk to the dead man." She grinned at the absurdity of what she'd just said, and Rory's confused expression was priceless. "I mean, we'll let her and Marie have a seance to communicate with Lou and see just who's interested in the whole process. I'm betting that once the killer finds out we have a package that Lou *mailed to himself*, they'll come creeping out of the woodwork trying to find out what's inside," she finished.

Rory pursed his lips, trying to think of an argument against her idea, but he had to admit, it sounded pretty good. "You've got to tell Emmett," he countered, "but otherwise, that crazy plan might just help the police figure out who killed Mr. Ross."

Annie smiled. "It might just help them catch them, too. Now I just have to go let my mother know that she can have her little spiritual communication session, and I have to make sure all the guests know that the dead guy got a package in the mail."

Rory shook his head in mock disbelief and grinned at Annie. "That sounds like a plan, Annie Purdy, and a darned good one, too."

They headed out of the barn and back towards the house. Annie felt certain that she could figure out who killed Lou Ross once she saw her guests' reactions to her revelation about the package. She just hoped Emmett wouldn't be too mad at her for taking things into her own hands in order to do so.

21

Planning a Seance

If it hadn't been for the fact that Emmett Barnes was completely smitten with Bessie Purdy, Annie would have never even considered using the dead man's jewelry box to try and tease out his killer. Since the Chief of Police was so fond of Annie's mother, she felt at liberty to ask him outright if she could 'borrow' Lou Ross's package in order to carry out her plan.

Of course, to anyone else, the idea would seem ludicrous and incredibly foolish, especially since there was no way of knowing how Lou's killer might react. However, Annie had begun to realize that life was too short for being sensible. She'd wasted many years in a 'sensible,' loveless marriage with a man who had, in the end, carried on his own fantastically impractical love affair right behind Annie's back.

Buying Rosewood Place had been Annie's first big risky act after she became a widow, but something told her that it wouldn't be her last. While she wasn't precisely ready to don leathers and join a motorcycle gang, or jump out of any airplanes, for that matter, she was beginning to feel that being a rebel sometimes could be a wonderful thing.

Because Emmett wouldn't want to see his darling Bessie's

only child thrown in jail for such a tiny thing as opening a package that wasn't strictly hers, Annie felt fairly confident about sharing her plan with him. She hadn't felt confident enough to actually do that in person--telephones were great for the cowardly advancement of bold plans--but she did at least let him know what she was planning, which kept her on the right side of the law, as far as she was concerned.

"Hmmm." That was the first and only thing that Emmett said after Annie's brief, breathless explanation of her plan. She could practically hear him twisting his mustache while he thought of how to reply, and she imagined him fussing at the facial hair so much that it would eventually just fall off altogether.

"Well, Annie, you know that tampering with someone else's mail--especially mail belonging to a murder victim in an ongoing murder investigation--is bad juju. Plus, it's illegal. However, since your name was on the package, we'll say, for speculating purposes, that it would be fine, under normal circumstances." She could tell he was trying to talk himself into allowing her to carry out her plan, but she worried that he would talk himself right out of it.

"Emmett, I promise I will keep an eye on the box. I don't even have to open it for the seance." The absurdity of what she'd just said made her want to laugh, but she held it in.

Emmett sighed loudly on the other end of the phone line. "I don't know what's worse, the fact that you taped the darned thing back up as if you never touched it, or the fact that you're letting that crazy woman fool your mama into thinking she can talk to dead people." He paused, trying to think of a gentle way to phrase his next statement. "You do know what's next, don't you? She'll have your mama thinking that she can talk to your daddy again." The accusation was a gentle one, but Annie felt its sting just the same.

"Emmett, I can't help what my mother believes, and although I doubt very seriously that Marie Robichaud can do any of the things she claims she can, she could help us lure out the murderer. If any of my guests start acting, well, weirder than they already do now," she promised him, "We'll know who killed Lou Ross."

Annie had ended the call feeling fairly positive about the whole situation. Emmett hadn't threatened to come and arrest her or even confiscate the package, though he did tell her that she shouldn't let anyone touch the jewelry box itself or damage the package. She supposed that the box's origins might yet have clues about Lou's past and those poor victims he scammed out of money.

Emmett had told her that most of his leads--including those from the laptop, which had been accessed but had proved frustratingly free from any helpful information--had led to dead ends. Lou Ross, it seemed, had also been Jerry Garrity, Emile DePascal, and Bob Smith at various points in time. As for his victims, those still remained a mystery, though Emmett still held out hope that he could identify a few by comparing them to police records in other states.

Annie wondered about the accomplice that had been working with Lou. Did anyone at Rosewood Place seem like the type of person who could lie and cheat innocent people out of their money?

Her mind drifted back to Frank Martin. A nagging thought reminded her that if he had killed Lou out of anger and revenge, the seance wouldn't necessarily tell her that. But would he be uncomfortable with the idea of Marie talking to the man's ghost and asking about his murder?

Annie reached down and unlocked her desk drawer to verify

that the package was still inside. It was, but she felt very anxious about keeping it in the office. If anyone were to come inside--and she was sure that people had been in here without her permission because they kept letting that darned cat in--the box would be vulnerable. She imagined the drawer's lock was simple enough to pick, but she didn't really have a better place to hide it, did she?

Annie closed the drawer and locked it once again. She'd have to just make sure that no one came into the office, and that would mean keeping the guests together and entertained until Marie could organize the seance. She picked up the clipboard with the guest information on it. Tomorrow Rob and Kizzy were due to check out. Mr. Alexander would leave, too. She realized that she'd never organized the cookout that she'd wanted to have for her guests. There was no time like the present, she supposed, and she'd already started mentally making her shopping list as she backed out of the little office and locked the door behind her.

She could hear Bessie in the kitchen, humming loudly and moving things around. The older woman didn't hear her daughter approach, and she jumped when she turned to find her giggling quietly. "Oh, for goodness sake! You scared me to death, just standing there like that!" She put her hand on her chest for dramatic effect. "Make a little noise, next time, will you?"

"Sorry, Mama. I thought you heard me. Listen, I want to run something past you." Annie pulled out a chair at the small dining table that sat on one side of the kitchen and motioned for her mother to sit. She sat down opposite her and put her hands palm-down against the cool surface of the table. "I've been thinking that we should do this seance thing after all. I talked to Emmett and Rory and they both agree that it could help us shake things up a little, maybe draw out Lou Ross's killer."

Bessie's face shifted through a few emotions. Happiness, relief, slight embarrassment, and finally confusion. "But what about the package? Did Emmett agree to let you use that? Marie said we'd need something that definitely belonged to the dead man in order for her to contact him."

"It's all been cleared by Emmett, but with one caveat. He says we have to make absolutely sure that nobody opens up the package or messes with it in any way."

"What do you think is in there?" Bessie asked.

Annie hated lying to her mother, but she didn't want her to know that she'd opened the box by mistake. "Whatever it is, I'm hoping that it lures the killer out." She explained her theory about the murderer looking for something in Lou's car and being unable to find it.

Bessie nodded her head. "I guess it makes sense. It might raise suspicion if you left an inn because a complete stranger died accidentally while you were there. But, what if the killer wasn't looking for something that belonged to Lou? What if the killer was someone else, like one of his victims?"

Annie was caught off-guard by her mother's statement. "I thought you said that you didn't think the Martins were capable of doing something like that?"

Bessie looked flustered. "Not the Martins, just Frank. Annie, he has a terrible temper. Doris told me that he used to be so calm and peaceful, but since their incident last year he's been just awful. She told me that he practically got into a fistfight with a co-worker just a few months ago and that's part of the reason why they want to move so far away. They need a fresh start."

Annie's gut tightened, trying to feel out her mother's suggestion. Yes, Frank could very well have killed Lou Ross, but then again, so could any of the other guests.

"And, of course, there's always the possibility that the killer wasn't even one of our guests," Bessie added, though neither of the women actually believed that to be true.

"So you think it's a bad idea to have a seance?" Annie was beginning to get very flustered and frustrated with her mother.

"Oh, no, I think it's a good idea!" Bessie explained. "I just think it's also good to look at every single possibility. I adore the Martins, and I would completely understand where Frank was coming from if it was he who killed Mr. Ross," she reassured her daughter. "But, I just can't for the life of me see any of our other guests being so, well, so murderous!" Bessie threw her hands up in frustration.

"I was also thinking that we should invite all of our guests to participate in the seance." Annie continued from her original declaration. "If everyone here knows that Lou left something that he valued, then it might tempt the killer to show their hand."

Bessie shook her head. "Or it might just drive us to ruin," she said grimly. "Marie told you that the fewer people involved, the better. Besides, do you really expect someone like Mr. George to get involved in a seance? Or Frank, for that matter? And I know that Rob will just laugh at us," she added, a flush of crimson dotting her pale cheeks. Annie knew that her mother wanted to believe in Marie's abilities, but she also knew that Bessie was ashamed of herself for wanting to believe something so unbelievable.

"Let's let our guests decide if they want to participate. I'm planning a last minute dinner--a cookout--for tonight. We've got a few guests who are leaving tomorrow and I thought that after the week we've had, it might be nice to have a casual meal together before, well, before we let Marie do her thing."

Bessie glanced around the kitchen in mild horror. "But, I've

178

nothing planned for a cookout!"

"We were having meatloaf anyway, so let's just use that ground beef for burgers and throw on a couple of packs of hot dogs. I can send Rory to the store for anything we don't have, and you won't have to cook," she added cheerfully. "Sound good to you?"

Bessie relaxed a little upon hearing that Annie had everything planned out. "I suppose I could make a peach cobbler," she replied slowly. "I guess it'll have to do."

Annie bit back a laugh at her mother's irritability. Bessie struggled to give up control of the cooking duties, and Annie suspected it had more to do with her mothering instinct than it did with her actual love of cooking.

"I'll let everyone know that we'll eat at six. Why don't you tell Marie she can use the dining room for her, umm, ritual? I'll set up the food on the back veranda, buffet-style. People can just help themselves."

"Are you going to tell them about Marie's plan?" Bessie asked, hoping that Annie would be the one to tell the guests so that she wouldn't have to do it herself. It was one thing to want to see the psychic's abilities in action, but quite another to admit to everyone else that she actually might believe in them.

"Okay, yeah, I can tell them," Annie conceded. "You just find out what Marie needs and we'll make sure this goes off as smoothly as possible."

It didn't take long to get Rory on board with the afternoon's plan. His only response to her confirmation that the seance would definitely happen was a shaking head and hearty chuckle. "I guess that's one way to lure out a killer," he joked.

After he'd left for the grocery store with Annie's shopping list and Devon riding along for company, Annie returned her attentions to the house. The sitting room bustled with activity as

Frank and Doris showed Kizzy and Bessie a selection of photos and printouts from their day of househunting. Doris seemed to have several houses that she loved; Frank seemed more enamored with the blue plate special he'd eaten at the Barbecue Shack.

With half of her guests in the same place all at once, Annie decided to mention the evening's planned events. "I hope you all saved some room for some home-cooked hamburgers," she announced, trying to sound as cheerful and relaxed as possible. "We're cooking outside this evening and have a full spread. I thought it might be nice to have one last big hurrah before you all start heading off back to your homes," she explained.

"Oh, that sounds lovely!" Doris intoned, "doesn't it, dear?"

Frank nodded enthusiastically. "Can't say I'll complain about eating so well," he laughed.

"And afterward, for those who are interested," she continued, measuring her words carefully, "Marie will be showing us what she does for a living."

Annie expected some confusion after she made her statement, but she didn't expect the complete silence that filled the room. Even Bessie kept quiet, which was completely out of character for her mother.

Kizzy finally broke the stillness. "Oh, wow! You mean she's going to do a seance?" Annie realized that the blonde wasn't as ditzy as she looked. "Do you actually believe in that?"

Annie smiled at her guests. "I'm not really sure what I believe," Annie admitted, "but she seems convinced that she can communicate with Mr. Ross and find out more about how he died. I know that some of you may not want to participate, so I wanted to be upfront about the whole thing beforehand."

Kizzy thought over Annie's response for a moment. "Count me in," she replied finally. "I would love to know how that guy ended up in your pond. I mean, the police won't let me have my phone back, since it's technically evidence, so I might as well get something out the whole thing, right? It might be fun."

Annie expected Doris and Frank to protest, but to her complete surprise, Doris was excited by the prospect of watching Marie communicate with the dead man. "Oh, it's just like one of those television movies where the psychic solves the crimes! I love those--count me in!"

Frank rolled his eyes. "Count me out. I've got better things to do than listen to some phony psychic mumbling and moaning to the 'spirit world.' No thanks, Annie. I'll just hang out with the normal people, thanks."

"I think you're probably not the only one who'll feel that way," Annie confided, "but I wanted to invite everyone."

He laughed. "Can you believe my wife buys into all that stuff? She and your mom even swapped some recipes with that hooey-phooey psychic. Doris says she's going to start making her own beauty creams thanks to Marie. I guess I should thank her for that," he added. "It'll save me a fortune."

Annie looked baffled. "What kind of recipes did Marie give you, Mother?"

"Oh, they're not really recipes," Bessie replied, "are they Doris? I'm not sure what you'd call them. It's more like blends--essential oils, that sort of thing."

"Lavender, peppermint oil, that sort of thing," Doris confirmed. "You know, you can use almost any kinds of oils for blending," she told her husband, who showed his disinterest by faking a yawn and pretending to fall asleep.

Bessie held her hand out to Annie, inviting her to touch it. "I made some hand cream using some of her advice," she said. "Feel how soft it made my hands."

Annie agreed that her mother's hands were soft. She sniffed them, breathing in a blend of fragrances. "Mmm, is that lavender and roses?"

"Smells good, doesn't it?" Bessie asked. "Marie gave me a list of all kinds of oils I can use and the things I can treat with them," she added. "She even let me try some of her own blends," she continued.

Annie realized that this was probably why she smelled such strange aromas whenever Marie was around. The woman was probably drowning in all the essential oils and incense fumes.

"Well, I'm going to leave you guys to your house-hunting. I'm going to let the other guests know about dinner and see if Marie needs anything for her, um, well, I'll just see if she needs anything."

Annie left the sitting room and its guests and made a beeline for the dining room. She hoped that Marie wouldn't do anything crazy like insist on lighting a hundred candles or burning a dozen sticks of incense in there. She didn't find Marie in the room, but she did find that the dining table had been carefully covered with an old tablecloth. There were candles, but not a hundred of them. Instead, three large pillar candles lined the center of the table. They were unlit but looked as though they'd been used many times before.

Annie was surprised at how simple the setup for a seance seemed to be. She wondered whether Marie would have other requirements or bring out anything else when the actual process began. A sound behind her in the hallway made Annie jump.

"Did you bring me the package?" Marie asked in a quiet, calm voice.

"Oh, Marie, I didn't hear you," Annie replied. "I don't have it with me, but I'll bring it when it's time for the--well, when everybody comes in here and sits down."

Marie smiled, but it wasn't a friendly smile. Instead, it looked slightly vacant, like the psychic had already begun reaching out and communicating with the spirits. She didn't seem to be quite wholly on the same plane, let alone planet, as Annie. "Everyone?"

"I invited our other guests to join in. I hope you don't mind, but they want to help Mr. Ross as much as you do," she lied.

Marie blinked. "The more, the merrier," she replied. "Now, if you'll excuse me, I'll be in my room until the ceremony begins. I need to rest; it's very tiring communicating with the dead."

She was gone before Annie could formulate a response. Annie pulled the door to the dining room closed behind her as she left the room, then she went upstairs to try and find her remaining guests. She had a feeling that Rob would want to be present during the seance, but she genuinely had no idea how Mr. George would react to the whole thing.

As she wandered through the halls of her home, Annie hoped and prayed that the evening's activities would prove productive. If her theory was right, she could lure out Lou's killer and help the police make an arrest. Of course, if her plan didn't work, she'd have to spend at least one more night sleeping under the same roof as a cold-blooded killer.

22

A Dead Man's Face

The weather was perfect for outdoor cooking. It was, Annie believed, even nicer than the first day that her guests had arrived. That felt like a lifetime ago, despite the fact that it wasn't even a full week. Still, when the days were filled with dead bodies, unexplained fires, and dramatic illnesses--all of which seemed to relate directly to her guests--Annie began to second-guess her choice of careers.

If running a bed-and-breakfast is going to be this exciting, she mused, *maybe I ought to raise our rates.*

Rory returned from the store with everything Annie had requested, plus a few items Devon had insisted that his mom wouldn't mind him buying. Annie glanced at the receipt. "What's this fifteen dollar gift card?" she asked.

"I needed some new apps?" Devon shrugged, then added, "But they're for school, so it's all good."

Annie doubted that this was completely true, but she decided to let it slide this one time. She realized with a start that her son would be starting school in a little over a week and she hadn't even had time to read over the school handbook. In New York, Devon's school had a uniform. Here in Coopersville, uniforms were unheard of, but she was pretty sure that the dress code had changed since her days at school.

"Devon, remind me to double-check your school supply list this weekend. I want to make sure you have everything you need before they pull all the school supplies from the store shelves and put the Christmas decorations up," she grumbled. "Hey, that reminds me, did you get a box of school supplies out of my office?"

Devon made a face. "Ugh. Why would I do that? I don't want to think about school at all until you drag me kicking and screaming through the front doors of the high school, thank you very much."

Annie shook her head. "I must have just put it somewhere and forgotten about it. I guess it will turn up," she added. "Why don't you put Karma out in the barn while we cook and eat? If you wash your hands, you can help Rory cook," she added.

Devon thought this over for just a moment. "Can Karma have a burger?"

Annie closed the refrigerator, where she'd just stashed the large tub of coleslaw that she'd had Rory pick up from the store. "Okay, but no bun. And only after all the guests have eaten," she added.

"And only if you give TigerLily some, too," Bessie said, breezing into the kitchen. She grinned at her grandson. "You wouldn't want to hurt her feelings, would you?"

Devon smiled back at her. "I know better than to upset the women in this family," he teased. "I'll go put the dog out and see if Rory needs any help firing up the grill."

As Devon left, Annie turned to her mother. "I think the guests seem to be pleased about the cookout. The weather's holding out for us, Rory's working his magic on the grill, and nobody seemed to be too upset by the idea of a seance," she said with a hint of hopefulness in her voice.

"Rory's not interested in being a part of the seance, I take it?"

Annie laughed. "No. And Frank's not interested, neither is Mr. George, but surprisingly, everyone else wants to do it."

Bessie nodded. "I could have told you that Alexander George wouldn't be interested. He's a man who only likes facts, I think. Not that that's a bad thing, mind you, but I like to keep my mind open to all possibilities," she said.

Annie couldn't help but think that her mother liked to do more than just 'keep open to possibilities,' but she kept this opinion to herself. Let her mom believe in supernatural things, if she liked. As long as there was no harm in it, the woman deserved to have a little fun.

They finished putting away the various items of shopping, then Annie watched as her mother went through the process of making a gallon of sweet iced tea. As the teabags were brewing on the stove, Annie's phone rang in her pocket. Emmett's number filled the screen.

"Hello?" Annie knew that her mother would want to talk to Emmett if she knew who was on the other end of the line.

"I've had an idea," he replied, not bothering with a greeting. "Go check your fax machine. I'm sending a copy of the photo on Lou Ross's driver's license. I thought it might shake things up a little if you set it out during your mystical woo-woo session," he added, barely disguising a chuckle.

"You think it might make the killer a little uncomfortable, make it easier to tell who killed him?" she guessed.

"Maybe. Can't hurt. I'm sending a couple of cars up your way, by the way. They won't come to your place, but they'll be close, just in case."

Annie hoped he wasn't sending Delbert Plemmons. If it came down to Delbert catching the bad guy, she had a feeling that they would be sadly disappointed. He was a nice enough young man, but as far as police officers went, Annie felt Delbert was lacking most of the skills needed to do the job, like agility, attention-span, and a sense of direction.

"If you send Delbert Plemmons, please give him a partner who knows left from right," Annie teased.

"Ooh, is that Emmett?"

Annie realized that she'd given the game away by mentioning Delbert. "Yes, Mama, it's Emmett."

"Tell him I'm cooking fried chicken on Sunday," she said, hollering it loud enough for the man to hear on the other end of the phone.

"You heard that, right?" Annie asked.

Emmett chuckled, a sound like a cross between Santa Claus and Elmo from Sesame Street. "You tell your mama I'll be there with my eating pants on," he confirmed. "Annie, you be careful tonight." His tone changed so quickly, it threw Annie off-balance. "I don't want you trying to play hero, trying to stop any suspects. You just need to let me know who looks guilty and I'll have my boys swoop in and take care of the rest."

Annie thought his concern was sweet, but she also thought it was a little sexist. "I'll be fine, Emmett. You just make sure that Delbert doesn't trip over his shoelaces if he has to chase anybody, okay?"

With Sunday's dinner invitation confirmed and Annie notified about the police officers who'd be nearby, they ended the call with a promise that Annie would call Emmett if she had any reservations about the unusual plan. As soon as she'd ended the call, Annie headed for her office to retrieve the promised fax. She had a feeling that Emmett was right about the photo. After all, if you'd just murdered someone in cold blood, it had to be pretty disconcerting to have to look at the person while you tried to contact their ghost.

The photo from Lou's driver's license looked nothing like the man she'd pictured in her head. Although Annie had been the one to find his body, she'd never actually looked at Lou's face when the police and fire department pulled him out of the pond. Emmett had spared her from that gory job and she was grateful, but it kept Lou from feeling like a real person to her. Now, staring at his face looking back at her from the blurry black and white photo, she felt a twinge of sadness.

Here was someone's child, albeit a child who preyed on the insecurity and fear of others for financial gain. He looked so *ordinary*. Annie shuddered to think that Lou was the type of guy she would have overlooked if she'd met him out somewhere. He had the sort of mildly attractive, completely generic face that she reckoned all conmen should have, which is to say, he was wholly unremarkable.

Annie wondered what drove the man to his profession. Did he indeed have a mother in Mobile, waiting for a call from her son that would never come? Annie put that thought firmly out of her head. If Lou Ross had a mother, then Emmett would find her, and Annie didn't need to worry about a grieving stranger right then.

She checked the time on her phone and realized that Rory probably had the grill fired up by now. It would take a little while for the charcoal to hit just the right temperature, so she still had time to help her mother prepare the rest of the food for the dinner that she'd come to think of as a sort of 'going away' celebration. It was almost impossible to believe that the first week of business had almost finished. It seemed like only five minutes ago that she'd been painting, scrubbing, and helping Rory piece the place back together after years of neglect.

Annie looked around her as she left her office and headed for the kitchen. She fell in love with the old house a little more every day and couldn't imagine ever leaving it. She hoped her guests felt that way, too. Well, maybe she didn't want them to love it so much that they'd never leave, but she hoped that she'd created a wonderful enough place that they'd be tempted to return time and time again.

Annie could hear her mother's laughter ringing out from the kitchen before she ever set foot in the room, followed by Frank's booming voice and Doris's high-pitched squeal.

"And that was when I told them I was through," Frank laughed, wiping tears from the corner of his eyes. "Man, let me tell you, I will not miss having a full-time job, that's for sure."

"Oh, you'd be surprised how quickly being retired gets boring," Bessie replied. "Mind you, I didn't work full-time, anyways. Never had to, thanks to my Robert, but I still wanted to get out there and feel useful. I volunteered at the church for many years until he passed away, and then I guess I sort of shut myself off from all that." She sighed, "I love working at this place, though. Wouldn't trade it for the world, plus I have my Annie and Devon here with me. Couldn't ask for more," she finished.

Annie hadn't realized how isolated Bessie had been before she'd moved back home. Her mother had always given her the impression that her life was busy, but Annie supposed that she'd just been trying to alleviate Annie's guilt over not visiting more often.

"Mama," she said, making her presence known. "I just came to see if you need any help with the food."

"Oh, no, dear, I've got it all under control. Frank here was just telling me about his job. I do believe he's happy to be retiring," she added, and the trio burst into fresh laughter. Annie felt as though she'd missed the joke completely, so she just smiled dumbly.

"What's that?" Doris asked, wiping her eyes gently and pointing to the photo in Annie's hands.

"Oh, I thought that I'd put it out during the *seance*," she replied, still not wholly comfortable with the word. "It's a photo of Lou Ross," she explained.

"Oh," Doris let out a small gasp. "Can I see it?"

Annie passed Doris the sheet of paper and watched her carefully to gauge her reaction. It wasn't what she expected at all.

"Oh, such a shame," she clucked, "Look, Frank. Look how young he seems."

Frank took the image and nodded silently. He stared at Lou's face for a long minute, then passed the paper back to Annie.

"I just don't get it," he said finally. "That guy, he looks like a nice guy. Why would he go and con people out of their money? What's wrong with people?" He shook his head. "And who knows what the freak looks like who killed him."

"Well, it could look just like one of us," Doris reminded him. She put a hand on Annie's arm. "Thank you for showing this to us. It's so easy to forget that this dead man was someone's son, maybe someone's husband or brother. Regardless of what he did before he came here, he certainly didn't deserve to end up the way he did."

Frank agreed. "I know I ran my mouth off the other day, saying that he got what he deserved, but Doris is right. Nobody deserves that."

Annie looked at her mother, who had an I-told-you-so look on her face. If she'd ever doubted the Martin's innocence, you certainly couldn't tell.

The mood had changed completely in the cozy kitchen. Annie felt both relief that Frank and Doris seemed to have dropped off her suspect list and regret for having interrupted their vivacious laughter.

"I guess I'll go and check on Rory and Devon, see if they need anything."

Annie left them to get back to their chatter and headed outside. The scent of charcoal and lighter fluid made her feel both hungry and anxious. After the fire on the deck, Annie didn't think she'd ever feel the same about lighter fluid ever again.

Annie was surprised to find Alexander George sitting with Rory and Devon, a bottle of root beer in his hand and a smile on his face.

"Hullo, Annie! Did you come out here to make sure we weren't getting into any mischief?" her bespectacled guest asked.

Annie smiled back at him and made her way over to where the three of them were sitting in deck chairs beneath the shade of a large oak tree. "I can't see you three getting into any mischief," she replied, fanning drifting smoke out of her eyes. "I just thought I'd see if you needed anything," she said to Rory. "And I wanted to let you know that Emmett sent something over," she added, holding up the photo of Lou.

Devon was the first to ask about it. "Who's that?"

Annie explained about the photo, leaving out the part about using it to lure out Lou's killer. Alexander looked very uncomfortable when Annie offered him the photo. He took it with slightly trembling hands.

"This is the dead man?" he asked. "He was a bad man?"

His question surprised Annie. "Well, I suppose you could say that. The police think he stole money from many people." She glanced at Rory, who was studying Alexander's reaction to the photo very carefully.

Alexander's mouth made a firm line. He handed the image back to Annie. "I don't like looking at pictures of dead people, even bad ones. Does that mean that the person who killed him is a good person?" he asked earnestly.

Annie could see the confusion in Alexander's eyes. She also felt exceedingly uncomfortable with his last question. "Well, no, Mr. George, of course not. Killing is bad, regardless of what the dead person did before they died."

"If the killer is a bad person, why haven't they been caught?" He looked from Annie to Rory. "Do you think they'll kill someone else?"

Rory spoke up. "I'm sure that the police will stop them before that can happen, Alexander." He took the photo from the man's hands and passed it back to Annie. "Let's let Annie put this in the house so it doesn't get ruined."

Alexander didn't protest, he simply handed the photo to Rory and took a sip of his root beer. "I'm starving," he said randomly. "I can't wait for dinner."

Rory walked a few steps away from Devon and Alexander, motioning for Annie to walk with him.

"Do you think that his reaction was, um, normal?" Annie whispered.

"For him? Probably. But, I'll keep an eye on him, okay?" He glanced over at Alexander, who was now enthusiastically describing something to Devon, using his hands to illustrate whatever it was they were discussing. "I know he's weird, but I can't help but like the guy. It's like--it's like he just has no filter, you know?"

Annie trusted Rory, and she wanted to trust his judgment on Mr. George, but the strange man in the wiry spectacles made her feel very uncomfortable. "Don't leave him alone with Devon, okay? Just in case."

She thought that she could see the slightest hint of a frown, a touch of disappointment in Rory's face. "Okay. I'll keep an eye on him."

As she walked away, Annie could hear their discussion pick up again. Devon laughed loudly at something Rory said and she could hear Alexander complain that he didn't get the joke. Annie began to wonder whether Rory hadn't been right about the odd little man. Maybe he was some sort of autistic savant, or at the very least, someone who simply took everything literally.

Kizzy and Rob drifted downstairs and out on the veranda shortly after Annie's conversation with Rory. She showed them the photo and wasn't surprised by either guest's response.

"I know that the police said he was a bad man," Kizzy confided to Annie, "but I can't help but think about how sad the whole situation is. I mean, if he was on his way to visit his mother, well, what's she going to think when he doesn't turn up? And Rob told me that the police haven't been able to figure out who she is or where she lives--it's so awful."

Annie chewed the inside of her cheek just a little upon hearing how much Rob already knew about the police investigation. "What can I say?" he shrugged when she mentioned it to him. "I'm just lucky Emmett likes me. I've pretty much pestered the crap out of him this week, trying to get a lead that might break the case."

"Rob, you're not a detective. You're a reporter and a very good one, but I think you should be careful about trying to solve Lou's murder. After all, you know that so far, the police still suspect one of your fellow guests." Annie gave him a stern look, the kind she typically reserved for Devon when he did something she

193

considered foolish or dangerous.

Rob rolled his eyes, which made him look much younger than his late twenty-something age. "And you're not my mom. No offense," he added quickly. "I'm not trying to solve the murder. Well, I mean, if I happened to solve it while helping the police gather information, then, so be it." He crossed his arms. "And isn't this a case of the pot calling the kettle black? I mean, come on, what is this seance if it isn't a sting operation designed to lure out a killer using a mysterious package that just conveniently happened to arrive from beyond the grave?"

Now it was Annie's turn to cross her arms. "There was nothing convenient about it. And, yes, I'm aware that it looks a little like a sting operation, but mostly I just want to see who seems the most interested in Lou Ross's mysterious package." She arched one eyebrow. "You seem pretty interested in it. Should I be concerned?"

Rob's indignance was quick but short-lived. "I like you, Annie Richards. I'm not going stand here and argue with you. Point taken, I will be cautious and more discreet from here on out."

Annie relaxed her own stance. "I know you mean well. Now, go enjoy your food before Marie calls us in for her big event."

Rob and Kizzy walked, very closely together, Annie noticed, out to the veranda to get their food. Annie didn't feel very hungry. In fact, her stomach was in knots thinking about the seance. She'd never been to anything like that before, and she wasn't entirely sure how comfortable she felt letting Marie have one in her home. Even if it was a load of hogwash, the idea of possibly sitting around the table with Lou's killer while trying to communicate with his departed soul gave Annie a proper case of the heebie jeebies.

23

Speaking With the Spirits

Annie wasn't the only one who didn't eat anything at dinner. Marie had locked herself away in her room, explaining cryptically that she needed to spend some time charging her 'psychic energy' and preparing herself mentally for the task of communicating with the dead. Annie wasn't sure what exactly one did to prepare for such an activity, but she imagined it involved a great deal of essential oils and incense, judging by the stink coming from the room.

I'm going to have to Febreeze the heck out of that place when she leaves, Annie fumed. She just hoped that the scent hadn't seeped into the walls and furniture. The room would only be empty for a couple of days and then a new guest would be arriving to take advantage of Annie's special low prices during her first month of business.

Everyone else ate plenty. Rory's dab hand with a grill meant that the burgers were juicy and tender, cooked nearly to perfection. He'd brushed the hot dogs with some tangy barbecue sauce while they cooked, giving them a sweet kick that had Frank going back for seconds and thirds.

Bessie had whipped up not only her promised peach cobbler,

but she'd managed to whip up a sneaky batch of banana pudding. Annie suspected her mother had begun the dish the day before--everyone knows banana pudding needs to 'set' for a good day to be any good--but she didn't say anything when Bessie proclaimed it a 'last minute' contribution to the evening meal.

MegaMart's coleslaw and potato salad were nowhere near as good as homemade, but the guests didn't seem to mind. Devon's contribution, several bags of potato chips, were also welcomed by the ravenous guests. After eating for what felt like hours, but was actually only like thirty or forty minutes, Annie's guests were full and content to sit out on the deck in the dappled sunlight that filtered down through the branches of the few oak trees that dotted the property.

Annie glanced at her watch every so often, keenly aware that Marie hadn't spoken to anyone for several hours. She was beginning to fear that the woman had fallen asleep or simply forgotten that she was going to perform a seance. If it wasn't for the fact that Annie could see the woman's compact little Honda sitting by the edge of the drive, Annie would have sworn she'd simply packed her bags and hit the road.

Finally, as the sky began to darken and conversation began to dwindle, Marie appeared like a specter at the back door of the screened-in porch. "It's time, Annie. Please bring me that which belongs to the dead man."

Marie was dressed head-to-toe in black. Her shirt was a plain turtleneck, quite hot for August, Annie thought, and her skirt was a voluminous, billowy thing full of layers. She was sure that Marie wore it to look more spectral, more mysterious, but the rail-thin woman only looked odd in the getup, like a stick insect stuck in a big, black marshmallow. Her pale face and hands stood out in stark contrast to the getup, and the resulting look was both startling and a little unnerving.

Bessie sidled up to her daughter. "She looks like one of those Barbie doll toilet paper covers," she whispered. "What is up with that getup?"

Annie shrugged. "I'm sure it's for effect. Let's get everyone seated in the dining room so I can get the package."

Everyone except for Rory, Devon, Alexander, and Frank headed up the small hill towards the house. "Give him my regards, won't you?" Frank hollered after them, chuckling at his own morbid sense of humor.

Annie noted that Devon had bolted straight for the barn the minute that she'd started towards the house. *Probably sneaking that dog another burger*, she mused.

The house was completely dark, at least the downstairs part. "Trust me," Marie explained when Annie mentioned it, "you'll want the lights out. Sometimes spirits can get, well, spirited. They love to manifest in light sources, and I've seen more than my fair share of shattered bulbs."

Annie and the others followed Marie wordlessly to the dining room where the three candles were now lit. They cast just enough light for everyone to see each other's faces, but no more. Annie was surprised by how dark the room was with all the lights out. The single window in the dining room was blocked by a heavy curtain, and the overall effect was creepy.

Annie waited for everyone else to be seated, then she made her way back to her little office, which was just down the hall from the dining room. She wished that she'd brought a flashlight, and once inside her office, she did turn on the light, but only long enough to unlock her desk and retrieve the package. After turning out the lights and closing up the office, she returned to the dining room and deposited the package unceremoniously onto the middle of the table. Then she pulled out the now-folded photo of Lou from her pocket and unfolded it, placing it so that it faced Marie directly.

The medium's eyes grew large for a moment. "Where did you get that?" she asked, pointing to the photo.

"The police sent it to me. I thought, well, I thought it might help you to focus if you knew what he looked like." Annie hadn't meant to upset the woman, but she could tell that Marie was uncomfortable with the image of Lou Ross staring back at her. Perhaps she didn't usually use a photograph to identify her spirits? "I can get rid of it, if you want."

Marie didn't say anything, but she nodded, and Annie retrieved the paper and returned it to her pocket. Then she took her seat beside Bessie, who was on Marie's left. Doris sat to Marie's right, with Rob and then Kizzy completing the circle. Because the table was a long rectangular one (meant to sit twelve or sometimes even sixteen people if they squeezed in just right), Rob and Kizzy were separated by an expanse of table. They strained their arms across its surface, reminded by Marie to keep touching each other.

"The spirit may try to inhabit you if you aren't touching someone else," Marie warned them. "I can handle that, but none of you are experienced with these sorts of things, and it could be very dangerous for you."

Bessie squeezed Annie's hand a little more tightly at this. Annie smiled reassuringly in the darkness and waited for Marie to begin.

The tall, thin, pale woman reached across the table and took the package in her hands. She ran long, spindly fingers across it, caressing the corners and, Annie couldn't be sure, but she thought she saw her sniff the address label. A low, humming noise filled the air, and Annie realized that it was coming from Marie.

"Come to us, Lou Ross. Come to us and tell us what you need for us to hear." She repeated this a few times, and Annie was beginning to feel beyond foolish when suddenly the flames on the candles began to flicker in an odd way. They seemed to twitch and bend, dancing in a random pattern that was wholly unnatural and more than a little spooky.

"I know that you're here, Lou. Come to me...speak to me!" Marie's voice rose to just below a wail. "I will speak with you now!"

A loud, low groaning noise filled the room, and Annie couldn't be sure if the sound was coming from Marie or somewhere behind her. Marie held the box gripped firmly in her hands, and she dropped her voice to a whisper. "Yes, yes, I see…" she trailed off, mumbling something that Annie couldn't quite understand.

Suddenly Marie stood, holding the package above her like an offering. She spoke, but her voice didn't sound like her normal one. It was growling and urgent. "I want what belongs to me!" Marie froze, her back arched in some sort of spasm, and then she screamed.

Then, the candles went out, and the room was thrust into a most complete darkness.

24

A Killer Takes the Bait

Annie had never completely understood the meaning of the phrase 'controlled chaos,' but her evening was about to become the complete definition of the term. A few seconds after the candles went out, there was a loud bang from somewhere behind Marie's chair, then the sound of breaking glass. The entire table shook, which caused Doris to withdraw her hand from Kizzy's.

"No, don't let go!" Kizzy shrieked. "I don't want to get possessed by a ghost!"

It took Annie a moment to get her bearings in the fully darkened room, but she had been listening intently from the moment that the candles went out, so she heard the scuffle of feet on the hardwood floor and what sounded like fabric tearing somewhere behind Kizzy's chair. She stood up, pulling her hand away from her mother's.

"Annie, what's going on?" Bessie sounded more than a little frightened. "Was that my antique pitcher I heard smashing?" Bessie's hearing was keener than her daughter's, Annie marvelled.

"I don't know. Marie? Marie, are you alright?"

Everyone hushed their whispers at Annie's question. She got no reply, only the sound of silence and her own heart beating in her chest.

"Rob, get the lights." Annie barked out the order even as she made her way around the table. A moment later the electric lights flickered on, causing everyone in the room to squint and cover their eyes. Annie wasn't exactly surprised to find Marie's chair empty, after all, she hadn't responded when Annie had called out. Annie was a little shocked and saddened to see that Bessie's guess about her antique ceramic pitcher was right. The decorative piece lay in fragments on the floor. *It must have been knocked over when Marie stood up*, Annie guessed.

"Where's Marie?" Bessie sounded surprised and a little hurt to find that the psychic was missing.

"And where's the package?" Rob asked, pointing to the empty space where the package should have been.

Annie and Rob both came to the same conclusion at once. He opened the door to the dining room, which had inexplicably slammed shut during the seance, and stepped into the darkened hallway. Annie darted out after him.

"Wait!" she insisted. "Let me check her room. Why don't you go and tell Rory to keep an eye out for her. If she tries to leave the plantation, he can stop her."

Rob agreed reluctantly to her suggestion. Annie felt her way down the hallway, flipping on lights as she went so that she could see. By the time she'd climbed the stairs and reached Marie's room, she had convinced herself that the woman would be gone, completely vanished. She put her ear to the woman's door, and listened. She could just make out the sound of muffled sobs.

Annie kept a master key to every door in the house. She pulled her keys from her pocket and selected it now, opening the door as quietly and as quickly as she could. She wasn't quite prepared for what she found, and for a moment, she didn't quite know what to say.

Marie had packed her bags and was obviously ready to leave. She was also on her knees on the floor, cradling the wooden jewelry box, its cardboard box ripped to pieces all around her. Bits of foam peanuts drifted in the air and clung to Marie's oversized skirt, which had a large tear in it. The woman turned to look at Annie. Her face was streaked with tears, and she clutched the box defensively.

"Marie, are you alright?" Annie felt lame, but it was the only thing that she could think to ask.

"What do you think? Do I look alright?" Marie spat the words at Annie. She glanced at her bags, and Annie realized that she'd almost let the woman slip away.

"Why did you take the box?" It was a command as much as it was a question, and Annie's hand went out instinctively, asking for Marie to hand it over.

Marie suddenly seemed more aware of the situation, of her disheveled state, and of Annie's insistence on having the jewelry box that Lou Ross had presumably meant for his mother to have. "I told you from day one that you should have had this place cleansed of the negative spirits." She rose to her feet. "I'm not through with this," she said simply, and Annie realized that she meant the box.

Annie realized with sudden clarity that she was in the presence of someone who was not in her right mind. "Marie, why don't you come downstairs and let me fix you up some tea. You've been through a lot, it seems."

Marie laughed. "You don't know the half of it!" She darted her eyes around the room, then scuttled over to her bags and snatched them up with one hand, the other still gripping the jewelry box tightly. "I'll be checking out now, Mrs. Richards," she said coolly, "I believe you have my credit card details--please charge my card accordingly."

Annie was blocking the door, but she stepped backwards just enough for Marie to pass. When the woman came closer, Annie held out her hand again. "The police are going to need that, Marie." Annie glanced down the hallway, hoping to see Rob or Rory, but she realized that they'd be watching Marie's car, waiting for her to make her escape.

Marie stopped, frozen in her tracks for a long moment. She cocked her head to one side and seemed to be listening to a voice that only she could hear. Goosebumps slipped down Annie's spine as Marie broke into a widening grin. "I'm not falling for that one. I'm getting what belongs to me, Lou Ross, and no one is going to stop me."

One minute Annie was tensed, waiting for Marie to make a move. The next, she was falling backwards, her feet swept out from underneath her by one of Marie's bags. As the world spun backwards, Annie caught a glimpse of black fabric billowing out behind a running Marie, then all hell broke loose.

Fortunately for Annie, Marie's bag managed to make its way underneath her backside as she fell, breaking her fall somewhat and lessening what surely would have otherwise been a very painful fall. Unfortunately, it felt--and smelled--as though the bag was full of bottles of essential oils. Annie slipped as she tried to rise, and discovered an oily puddle of liquid oozing out of the bag. She pulled herself up along the wall and took off running after Marie, slipping only for the first few steps.

Before she'd reached the landing at the top of the stairs, she heard the barking, then the growling, and by the time she'd hit the first step, she heard the screaming.

Despite the wailing cries of one seriously deranged psychic, the scene could have been a funny one. Karma, small as he was, had the woman cornered in the parlour, her billowing skirt now tangled tight in his puppy teeth. The dog, which only weighed about twenty pounds, according to Dr. Fisher, had managed to stop the terrified woman in her tracks. Before Annie could reach the bottom of the stairs, Devon came tearing onto the scene, stumbling to a stop as he realized that his puppy had Marie's skirt in his jaws.

"Oh, crap, Mom, I'm so sorry! Let me put him outside!" Devon reached for the dog, but Annie stopped him.

"No!" She glanced out the window beside the front door and saw blue lights. "Go outside and tell Delbert or whoever it is to come in here and bring some handcuffs."

Devon bolted back through the kitchen, and Annie marched over to Marie. She snatched the jewelry box from the woman's shaking hands. Despite everything that had just happened, Annie was surprised to find that she didn't feel angry at Marie. In fact, when she saw that the woman's glasses had come off and were lying on the floor, Annie couldn't help but pick them up and place them in her now empty hands.

Annie reached down and calmed the dog, who now sat obediently at her feet. He didn't drop Marie's skirt, but at least he'd stopped the barking. He still let out a brave little growl every few seconds, though. Marie whimpered in response.

"Oh, Marie, why?" Annie couldn't quite wrap her mind around the evening's events. Of all the guests in the house, Marie was the last one that she'd suspected of being a killer. She was so *airy fairy*, so *woo woo*, that Annie had completely written her off as nothing more than a lonely, loony woman looking for attention.

"Because it belongs to me," she said simply. "Or, I thought it did. But it's empty, and Lou's dead, and now it's all gone so wrong." Her words melted into sobs, and as Delbert appeared in the doorway of the kitchen, Annie motioned for him to wait.

"I don't understand--did you know Lou Ross?"

"I--I loved him," Marie sniffed. "But he lied to me. And he took everything--all of my money--even after I helped him."

Annie thought about the crumpled piece of paper she'd found in her office. "You mean telling him about the Martins?"

Marie nodded. "He thought they might be someone he'd--he'd taken money from," she confessed. "We were a good team, but he was better. He fooled me," she nodded, then dropped her head between her knees and gave into another sob.

"Why did you kill him?" Annie asked, her voice gentler than before.

"He betrayed me. There was money," she whispered, "a lot of it. And I only wanted my share, but he laughed at me. He told me he didn't have it, but he'd kept it safe. And then he said he couldn't stay here. I think he thought that the Martins were someone else, but I told him that it was safe here." She bit her lip, holding back more tears. "He said he had someone else in Mobile. He told me that he only needed to collect something from you and then he'd leave. I got angry, and I know I shouldn't have, but I kissed him."

"You kissed him?" Annie was baffled. "How would that kill a man?"

Marie put her fingers to her lips. "I knew he was deathly allergic to peanuts," she admitted. "I had peanut oil on my lips. It's wonderful for the skin, you know," she added absentmindedly. "For a moment, it was perfect. He kissed me back, and it was literally breathtaking," she giggled, then her face turned somber again. "But it was all for nothing. I was sure he'd have the money in his car, but that stupid dog nearly tore my hand off when I tried to look. I had to chase him off with a stick," she explained.

"That's why he doesn't like you," Annie marvelled. "You killed his owner, then you, what? Beat him with a stick until he ran off?" Annie was beginning to lose her sympathy towards the woman.

"Oh, no, I would never do that! I love animals, even ones that bark and bite, but he had to go away so I could find what belongs to me," she emphasized. "I just chased him a little, then he ran off into the night. Of course, it's just my luck that Lou had hidden it somewhere else."

"It?" Annie was confused. "You mean your money?"

Marie nodded. "I worked for months with him, gathering information and helping him convince people to give him their money. We worked so well together, and I really thought…" she trailed off.

"You thought he loved you and was going to meet up with you here, for some sort of rendez vous?" Annie decided that she did feel sorry for the woman after all. Heck, Annie had been in sort of the same situation once, not the situation where she helped anyone con people out of their money, but she'd been betrayed by someone who claimed to have loved her. Her own husband had died and left behind a mistress who seemed to have spent more time with David Richards than Annie had, and she'd been married to him for nearly two decades.

Delbert gave Annie a questioning look, and she nodded, letting him know that he could now come inside and arrest Marie. As Delbert pulled out his handcuffs, Annie couldn't resist asking one more question. "Why were you so sure that he'd put the money in the package? Wouldn't that be risky? What if the package never arrived?"

Marie's face twisted with bitterness. "When you said that he told you to expect a gift for his mother, I knew. His mother died ten years ago."

Ouch. Annie decided that she did feel sorry for Marie. Whatever else she was, a bitter, heartbroken woman now sat on Annie's floor, and nobody should ever be lied to by someone who claimed to love them.

Annie gently pried the pup off of Marie's skirt and pulled him out of the policeman's way. The dog sat obediently at her feet as she watched the room begin to bustle with activity. People started filling the parlour, the guests from the seance who'd been left waiting for Annie's return, Frank searching for Doris, and Rory, who made his way straight to Annie's side.

"I'm sorry about the deck," Marie said suddenly. "I--I thought that I could somehow burn away the memory of that night, and I needed to convince you to do the seance. I had to be sure--" She stopped talking as Delbert began his speech about the right to remain silent, but as soon as he'd finished, Marie spoke again.

"Wait," she said to Delbert before he could push her through the front door. "Annie, Rose says 'thank you.' She told me that you know her secret, but you've kept it for her, and she really appreciates it. She wanted me to tell you that, and also to tell you that your father loves you very much."

Delbert waited for her to finish speaking, then pushed her out the door. "Nobody wants to hear your nonsense, lady."

Annie paled slightly. "Can you believe the nerve of that woman?" Rory asked her. "Even as they're hauling her away, she's trying to play on your emotions."

He noticed the box in Annie's hands. "Is that it, the package from Lou Ross?" She nodded. "Can I see it?"

Annie handed him the box. "I guess the police are going to be mad because it's covered in fingerprints now," she said. "Marie seemed to think that it was going to be full of cash," she added, "but it's empty."

"Did you check her pockets?" Rory teased. "And your silverware drawer?"

Annie shook her head. "She was so sad. I mean, she really seemed to love that guy, and according to her, he just crapped all over her from a dizzying height." She explained what little she knew about Marie's and Lou's working relationship, and their personal one. "He was a con artist in every single sense of the word, I guess."

Rory turned the box over in his hands, studying the craftsmanship. "This is weird," he muttered, fingering a seam along the base of the box. He shook the whole thing gently, then tapped the base with his finger. "It's got a hollow base," he whispered, "I'm sure of it." Rory continued to examine the box for a minute, until a familiar voice boomed from the kitchen.

"Annie, you in there?" Emmett appeared in the doorway to the parlour, his expression neutral. "Heard you had some problems with a guest?"

"Hey, Emmett," Annie called back. "Yeah, but it's okay, Karma caught up with her." Annie reached down and picked up the puppy, who rewarded her with wet doggie kisses.

"Is that important?" Emmett asked, pointing to the box in Rory's hands. "Like, 'belonged to the dead man' important?" He frowned at her. "I thought you told me you weren't going to open it."

"I didn't," Annie explained. She told him about Marie and the seance, and about Marie's relationship to Lou. "I really don't know why she stayed here all this time," Annie finished. "I only got that package a couple of days ago, so she couldn't have known about it before then. Why stay and risk getting caught?"

"Love and money. They make people do stupid, crazy things, Annie." Emmett shook his head. "What's in the box?"

"Noth-" Annie began, but Rory cut her off.

"About fifty-thousand dollars, I reckon." He held out the box for Annie and Emmett to examine. A panel on one side had been slid out to reveal a neat little drawer just the right size for stashing a stack of cash, and inside was a stack of hundred dollar bills about as thick as a paperback novel.

"Well, now," Emmett replied. "Wasn't expecting that." He took the box filled with cash. "I guess the psychic didn't see that coming, either, did she?"

Annie knew she'd have to make an official statement, but first she wanted to get the dog outside and go check on her mother. She left Rory talking to Emmett and started picking her way through the group of people that filled the parlour, carrying the dog outside to take care of his business.

25

All's Well and Farewells

The sun was shining through a spackling of clouds, put there, Annie was sure, to remind her just how spectacularly blue the Carolina sky could actually be. She carried two mugs of coffee, one with extra cream and sugar, and made her way down the slightly worn path to the wooden deck.

Bessie was there already, nibbling the edges of a cinnamon roll and contemplating something. Annie sat her mother's coffee down on the table beside her and fell into the empty chair on the other side of the little table between them. She took a large swig of her own coffee and sighed. *Bliss.*

Crickets chirped somewhere around them, and something splashed in the water's edge, probably a frog. Annie listened just a little harder and heard the gentle trickle of a stream. Actually, it was more like the remnants of one, that fed into the pond from some yet-to-be-discovered source. The scent of lavender and peppermint oil drifted on the air, probably from Bessie, since she'd used the oils just that morning to try and achieve a sense of calm and clarity.

For a few minutes, neither woman spoke. They just sat, enjoying the stillness of a new morning and the company of someone they loved. Finally, Bessie broke the silence.

"I still can't believe that Marie killed that man."

Annie nodded. "Mm-hmm. I know what you mean. I always thought she was just, well, you know, sort of *odd*, but not odd enough to kill someone."

"And she was a thief." Bessie said this matter-of-factly, but not with malice. "Emmett found that box of school supplies in her room, for goodness sake. Now, what would she want with those?"

"I think she was looking for the other package, the one with the money in it, but she got the wrong one," Annie explained. She recalled the number of times that she'd found her little office in disarray and blamed it on the cat. Emmett had told her that Marie, whose actual name was Emily Mortenson, had been arrested for breaking and entering when she was younger. Apparently 'Marie' knew how to pick almost every lock in Annie's house.

"And she set fire to the deck," Bessie added, taking a sip of coffee. "And poor Rory had to fix it," she added. She took a bite of her cinnamon roll and chewed thoughtfully. "But still, she was very nice to me."

Annie wanted to remind her mother that the 'very nice' woman had also stolen Alexander George's eyedrops and put them in Rob and Kizzy's drink, causing them to be violently ill. Emmett had confirmed that the same stuff used in eyedrops had been found in the tea. Annie could only surmise that 'Marie' had done this to make Frank look guilty, or perhaps to point the finger of suspicion at Alexander himself. She shuddered as she recalled finding the plastic cap to the bottle of eyedrops. Annie could never in a million years have guessed that she'd just found the evidence of a poisoning that day.

"She was a con artist, Mom. Her job was making people like and trust her. We all fell for it, I think." Annie thought about the way that her mother had been taken in by the woman. "Did she tell you that she could talk to dad?" Annie remembered the way her mother had been holding her father's binoculars that day on the veranda, as though she were embarrassed to have brought them out after so long.

Bessie pursed her lips. "I didn't ask her," she said quietly. "I wanted to, but I didn't want to, if that makes sense."

Annie nodded. "It does." She felt the same way, if she was completely honest with herself. Of course, she'd love to think that her father waited for them beyond the veil of everyday life, a shadow who watched over them and was always present. But if someone had faked that presence, or even completely debunked the possibility of it, she thought it would be just like losing him all over again.

"Kizzy and Rob are leaving today," Bessie said, out of the blue. "And I think Mr. George is going, too."

Annie smiled as she thought of Rob and Kizzy leaving together. Apparently the pretty actress had offered to give Rob a lift home, since he'd been dropped off by his cameraman when he first arrived. She hoped that they would continue to spend time together. They seemed to really enjoy each other's company and they were quite a cute young couple.

"Frank and Doris will be here for another day, maybe two," Annie replied, trying to look on the bright side. "You'll be able to visit without having so many people to cook for," she suggested. "And we have new guests coming next week. We'll be busy," she mused.

"Oh, I think so," Bessie agreed, though Annie sensed that she'd be sad to see their first guests leave. "What a week this has been," Bessie exclaimed. "A little more excitement than I would have liked..." She trailed off and hugged her coffee mug to her lips.

They sat in silence again for a few minutes. Annie was thinking of everything that needed to be done at the house that day, and Bessie was lost in her own thoughts. A flutter of wings nearby drew their eyes up to a pretty little red bird. It landed gracefully in the low branches of a nearby oak tree, and both women found themselves smiling.

"Our visitor is back," Annie noted.

"I'm not sure he ever left." Bessie smiled, and closed her eyes. "I don't need anyone to tell me that your father is still with us," she said quietly. "He's here, I'm sure of it."

Annie watched the little bird for a minute. "I'm sure you're right, Mama." *I'm sure you're right.*

If you enjoyed this book...

Please consider leaving a review! And if you'd like to receive updates about my future releases, please visit www.rubyblaylock.com and sign up for updates!

The Rosewood Place Mysteries

Bodies & Buried Secrets

When Annie Richards finds herself widowed at the age of 40, she leaves her home in New York City and returns to the small South Carolina town she grew up in. Hoping to create a new life for herself and her teenaged son, Annie teams up with her mother, Bessie, to buy a run down old plantation which they plan on turning into a beautiful bed and breakfast.

When an old enemy of Annie's turns up on her doorstep demanding that she sell her new home, Annie is determined to keep the woman from destroying her new dream. When the woman winds up dead in Annie's kitchen, it looks like the dream has become a nightmare as the police begin to suspect not only Annie but her contractor, Rory, as well.

Rory has a past that involves a stay in prison for assault and a high school romance with Annie. Will she let her old feelings for him cloud her judgment, or is he actually capable of murder?

And why do people seem to think that there's some sort of buried treasure on the plantation's overgrown, long-vacant grounds?

Annie finds herself in the middle of a deadly treasure hunt that could end up costing her more than just her new bed and breakfast--it could cost her her life, too.

The Carly Keene Cozy Mysteries

Dead Before the Wedding
Gravely Dead
Love, Death & Christmas Cookies
Can't Beat a Dead Horse

SIA information can be obtained
w.ICGtesting.com
in the USA
081213091218
22LV00019B/1021/P